MW00962426

COUNTDOWN
TO
DEATH

Iain McChesney

WAYZGOOSE PRESS

ISBN 10: 1938757181
ISBN 13: 9781938757181

Published in the United States by Wayzgoose Press.
Edited by Dorothy E. Zemach.
Cover design by DJ Rogers.
Cover review quote from Stephenie Sasse,
http://muttcafe.com/2015/09/countdown-to-death/

For my parents; and Elaine.
That growing up was weird enough to make
writing this sort of thing possible.

Table of Contents

Foreword

I DON'T RECALL THE FIRST TIME I HEARD THE NAME AGATHA Christie, but I know I was young. Was it from a dramatization on the BBC overheard while I hid behind our velvet couch? The suspense was killing me even then. I remember a trip to London with my mother—in my head I am seven or eight, being dragged out of Hamleys toy shop in London and walking to the embankment. On the way we passed a theatre I now know as St. Martin's, where Christie's *The Mousetrap* was playing. I learned a new word that day: *whodunit*.

My sister, the reader, had dozens of Agatha Christies on her shelf, but I was twelve when I picked up my first, an American edition, from a paint-chipped shelf in Grade 8 English. The cover was an island and a skull, which did not lack for appeal. The title: *And Then There Were None*. That book, the very definition of popular, has had its critics. They have said it is too short, too simple, too stereotyped, too improbable, that the characters lack depth, that the motive is lousy. Its fans would say all that misses the point—the book is wonderfully entertaining. And it is.

Countdown to Death (I wanted to call it *Ten Green Bottles*, but the association to the childhood song, a staple of school trips in Britain, has no such cultural reference in North America), began four years ago at a dinner party in Toronto. Friends had recently been in Scotland and stumbled across 'this peculiar castle on an island called Rum.' Did I know of it? No, I did not, but I went and I learned. It was all there, its history and atmosphere, the perfect setting for a whodunit murder.

The island in *Countdown*—it never gets a name—is a blending of the malts. Physically it is half Rum and half Easdale, a much smaller island in Argyll. Taigh Dubh, where our guests are invited, is the real Kinloch Castle on Rum, with a twist of Hearst Castle in California. Both are worth a visit. There really is a ballroom with raised windows so no one could spy in on the depravities, and there really were greenhouses with alligators—the truth being strangest of all.

Edward Gorey's delightful alphabet, *The Gashlycrumb Tinies*, inspired Black's notes, and the very talented Steve Blincoe breathed life into the drawings.

Chapter 1
An Invitation

Ten green bottles hanging on the wall;
Ten green bottles hanging on the wall;
And if one green bottle should accidentally fall,
There'll be...

IT WAS ONLY A MATTER OF TIME.

'Miss Grace! Miss Grace! If you would be so kind?'

Eleanor Grace took the proffered pen and paper with a practiced charm. The young woman asking for her autograph had rough-skinned, nail-bitten hands. They were hands that scrubbed floors or peeled potatoes destined for a deep fat fryer. They were hands that counted out change in a worn purse; hands old before their time. They reminded Eleanor of her mother's hands. She pushed the sentiment down.

'Who should I make it out to, darling?' She was perfect lipstick before a bright white smile, everything her public expected even if she couldn't hide the wrinkles at her eyes.

Eleanor wrote with feigned intimacy in powerful curving strokes. She took her thank you's as given and hoped the girl would disappear, but the young woman produced a mobile phone and waved it in her face.

'Can I take a selfie with you? May I? Just one shot, that's all.'

'Certainly not, you little witch. I'll set the police on you.' Eleanor pressed the button to bring the car window up while the girl stood with her mouth hanging open. On the other side of the tinted glass, her driver moved the girl on. Eleanor lit another cigarette. It helped to pass the time.

You're not pulling them in like you did before. We need another backer.

Who did the company think she was? *Damn the studio and its little men.* All the money she'd made for them.

The letter had arrived two months ago—who sent letters these days? *Dear Miss Grace, I have always been an admirer.* Proper handwriting on bonded paper, the scratch of a fountain pen. Miss Grace liked old-school style. The wealthy Lord Black inviting her to an island—*his* island—almost as far from Hollywood as you could get, amongst the wilds of the Scottish Highlands. He was having a few friends up, he said, and she might know one or two of them. No media at all, not to worry. She'd heard of the island, of course, though she'd never seen the place. Hadn't one of those celebrity rock stars had her wedding there? Eleanor had turned to Google. Yes, a picture of Taigh Dubh castle and an appalling wedding dress. Should she go? A nobleman on his Scottish island throwing a party for a select few? The hills of Los Angeles were stubble brown, shrivelled up under water restrictions, and Eleanor hadn't been back to Britain in quite some time. She brushed the grain of the paper stock again. *Black and his wealthy friends.* Her calendar was perilously thin.

A couple of drinks in the VIP lounge and she had slept through half the flight. *You're not pulling them in like you did before. We need another backer.* Time to plough fresh fields? Eleanor would get what she wanted from all of them. In the end, she always did.

Her driver was finished at the pump, and he knocked on the window glass.

'Sorry, Madam for the interruption. Not another garage for quite a few miles.'

'If I'm bothered again by any of these urchins, I'll see to it that you are fired.' Eleanor dropped her cigarette out the window. The boat would wait for her.

⊂⊗⊗⊃

'Where to?' asked the railway ticket vendor on the other side of the protective glass, his accented voice further distorted by the crackle from the loose-wired speaker. There was a queue, there was always a queue; he was meant to go on break five minutes ago.

'Oban,' answered the customer, a large man wearing a coat in summer, a large man with a foreign tan.

The ticket vendor almost hid his annoyance; he shouldn't have to ask. 'Single or return?' he grumbled in something approaching intelligible English.

'I'm going to Oban. Oban return,' said the man, whom politeness would call 'big-boned'. The ticket vendor took the customer for a rugby player on account of the bend in his nose.

'Platform 6. Goes at 10.45. Thirty-seven pounds eighty off-peak return, or forty pound open if you like.'

'Forty pounds!' the customer objected.

The ticket vendor looked at the suitcase with its bouquet of airport tags. He'd known the man was English with the first word out of his mouth.

'Been out the country long, have we, mate?'

The customer paid the fare in cash.

Inspector Henry Vail had never been to Scotland; he did not care if he never returned. Glasgow Airport via Singapore and Dubai, and then a taxi sweating of fried food and beer commuted him and his jet-lag to the city. He lifted his bag and put it on the rack above him and sat down heavily. He was tired. He took up nearly all of two seats, but he had something of that look that warned off company, and no one attempted to sit beside him. Henry clawed away at the plastic wrapper that protected a wet tuna roll. He had managed to find a bottle of water amid the shelves of Coca Cola. He was surprised when the train left on time.

The 10.45 rolled north out of Queen Street through a chain of age-smoked tunnels. It gathered speed as it turned to the west, and then breached daylight alongside a river. Clydeside shipyards would have blocked his view if he'd been travelling a hundred years before; instead he admired the stain of post-war housing and the derelict patchwork of recession. Quay wharves stood unused, barren and oily, where warehouses must once have spilled trade. Convention centres jacketed in plastic which passed for architecture were moated by empty car parks. Vail noticed these things only to warm his disdain for a Britain he had long left behind. Inspector Henry Vail the emigré, Henry Vail the improved man. It brought him a great deal of satisfaction to think that Hong Kong could swallow this whole. The Pearl River was over a mile wide before it even reached the South China Sea; the short brown stream out the window to his left would not even show on a Cantonese map.

My dear Inspector Vail, the letter had started. It had been years since he'd had contact with Lord Black. Henry slid down the seat as fatigue overtook him; he would find out his answers soon enough. He gathered his coat about him and sank his hands inside its pockets, where he fingered the change from the ticket counter, not much; two ticket stubs, out and back; a torn receipt for the tuna roll; a paper-and-string wrapped parcel. The weight of the revolver gave him reassurance. *My dear Inspector Vail…* it smelt of trouble. Henry watched the mountains approach before he nodded off to sleep.

It was a woman's voice, a Scottish voice, the sort that you might find reading the news before turning the channel to something good—inoffensive and class androgynous. 'This ScotRail train will depart at 12.36. First two carriages for Oban; rear two only for Fort William. Please ensure you are in the correct part of the train. Do not leave any possessions unattended. This ScotRail train will depart...' The recycled message went on repeat. Charles Fotheringham, Charlie to all but the banks, stepped out of the carriage. He looked at the sign for... *How the hell do you pronounce that?...* Crianlarich station, its gibberish equivalent in Gaelic underneath.

The platform was a fork in the road between the Argyll hills, and there was nothing about him but mountains. Apparently they were waiting for the Edinburgh train before they joined up and pushed off for Hogwarts. Charlie took the opportunity to stretch his cramped legs. He had been sitting too long, months it felt, and he had the urge to walk. The crunch of pebbles beneath his brogues made a satisfying noise.

The agency had been very clear; Lord Black was a busy man. Charlie had been selected on the merit of his previous works. 'Oh, yes?' he had asked. 'Which ones?' *His* Country Magazine *articles? His series on seashore birds? His pieces on rehabilitating veterans?* The agency was not at liberty to say. Do your research. Understand the man. He will be available for interview a month from now, at which time you will be given the location and expenses. An envelope with his fee was produced. *Ten times that upon completion.* A slice of the royalties was in the contract, though biography sales were fickle. But Charlie wasn't in a position to turn down anything; lately he'd being staying with his sister.

A part of him still believed it was a mistake, that he'd landed this job by accident. He kept the agency's letter in his pocket like a traveller hangs onto a St. Christopher. It had done him good, beyond a doubt. Something to focus on. The four thousand pounds was long gone, however. Wolf from the door in hard times.

'We will email you closer to the time, Mr Fotheringham. We will want your first draft soon after your interview. His Lordship would also appreciate a list of questions in advance, though you won't be restricted by that. Lord Black expects nothing less than a soul-washing honest review. Are we clear?' Yes, he'd told them. *Clear as mud.* Only dirtied souls needed washing. The agency had never asked him, and so Charlie had never mentioned it—he'd never written a biography in his life.

Charlie spent his month in the British Library going back through the newspaper records. He pulled the Hansard listings for Parliament, he read the colonial press; stuff on Lord Black wasn't hard to find, it was making sense of it all that was difficult. Everywhere he read of the company, but almost nothing of actual man. Business takeovers. Expanded ventures. But no flavour of the real person. It was going to be difficult to write Black's biography without knowing what inspired the man. His frustration drove him to dig further back, to root out where Black came from. What is a man but his family? What is a man but the home he makes, and what does *that* say of the wanderer?—Lord Black, it was clear, moved around. Charlie's question list only grew longer, and too soon his month was over.

The summons came by email, with his train ticket attached. *The boat connects and there is only one sailing; please do not be late.* Lord Black finally had time for him, and all his questions would be answered. Charlie was going to the island. He packed enough to last the week.

'Any chance of a light, mate?' A dozen smokers amongst his fellow passengers shared his desire to perambulate. They were shortish, thin-faced people, most of them pale despite this week's sun. Charlie carried a Zippo with him for occasions such as this, though he hadn't smoked since leaving Iraq, and he obliged the young man. 'Thanks pal,' was his reward. Charlie imagined the young man's tattoos would look limp in twenty years. *The things age does to us.*

There was another tattoo he noticed too. Big fellow. Older bloke. Hard-faced with a rifle-butt nose, with Royal Marine cropped hair and carrying a camel hair coat. Charlie's eye picked it up out of habit: the man's sleeve rolled up, a regimental tattoo on his forearm—a regiment different from his own. The man passed his coat from one hand to the other, and like that it was covered up. *Fellow's got a few stories,* thought Charlie. *Does he try to forget his too?*

A pocket watch in a Dali painting; time hanging limp on a tree. *Best move on,* Charlie thought. The Edinburgh train appeared.

⬡⬡⬡

DB struggled from the helicopter, its slowing propeller blades pushing him about. DB's hips did not approve of the stairs; he was no longer a young man.

'God damn it!' he cussed above the noise. His southern Gulf drawl announced to everyone that he was from the United States. DB passed his cane to a female attendant who appeared behind him at the top of the stairs. 'Here, honey, hold this for me.' He fought to keep his hat as he managed the rest of the way. DB reached the tarmac and turned around. 'Now give it back down here.' DB's favourite stick was handed back according to his wishes, the slim young woman seemingly familiar with the gentleman's coarse treatment. 'Where the hell are we?' he yawled into his whiskers, snow-white like his hair. 'Where's that Lord Black at?' DB had something of the sea lion about him, and the moustache added to the effect. 'Who the hell's here to meet us? This don't look like no island to me!'

'I'm sorry, sir.' The pilot had come out to assist them. 'The island is in restricted air space, so this is as close as we can get.'

'Restricted? What the hell do you mean?'

'There's a Royal Air Force base just up the coast, which NATO uses for test flights. The island isn't too far off, but civilian air traffic is not allowed.'

The slim young woman jumped into the conversation before DB could get started on the pilot. 'I believe it is all in order, Mr Bowers, sir. There's a car that will take us to the boat.'

Douglas Bowers III—DB to the world—owned a chunk of news media Stateside and a fair shake of it in Britannia too. He had lunched with five Presidents, which he was fond of telling people. And he did not care much for boats. 'If I wanted to buy a damned island to *sail* to, I'd have picked one with sunshine and rum!'

⊂⊗⊗⊃

Ms Joan Hedringer did not think DB was as much of a bully as he let on, but there was no reason to provoke him either. The assignment had promised a holiday and a retainer of considerable size. The large white Range Rover collected them and then shot off down the rural road.

'There's a hint of an accent, Miss Hedringer, or am I mistaken?' she'd been asked at her interview.

'South Africa. A long time ago.'

'You certainly come with glowing references.' They had flipped through her CV. 'Mr Bowers has some medical issues...'

Ms Hedringer interrupted, making it clear: 'I don't wipe bottoms, but I can give injections. I had a diabetic once.'

DB took his pills at night, and providing he laid off the whisky, she saw no reason for any alarm. Joan didn't really think he needed a nurse at all; and, not unaware of her own feminine charms (or the gentleman's reputation), was deliberate in her modest dress and attentive to who was in the room. The rogue was in Scotland with a chequebook in hand to add to his collection of toys. Why shouldn't she enjoy a few weeks away and pocket the crazy money? Hand out a few pills, check a pulse alongside his schedule.

Joan Hedringer straightened her pleated skirt and

pressed the button on her doeskin gloves. She was aware of DB's eyes on her legs. Through the window she could see the water.

Sir Cyrus Gordon made his introduction to the breakfast crowd in the dining room of the Puffer Hotel. It was this ignominy or eat in his room, and he admittedly enjoyed the recognition. The hotelier, a wise owl, had reserved the best table at the bay window for the exclusive use of his personage. One could look through the double-glazing out over the Atlantic Ocean, and, on a clear day, such as this, see the distant island of Mull beyond the straights of Jura. Before that, though, stood the Inner Hebrides: Muck, Muig, and Aardshan, inhospitable and charming. They were Gaelic names, conferred beyond the reach of Roman civilization, picnicked thereafter by Viking and Christian.

No one in the room had a care for that view, however, because celebrity drew all eyes. Sir Cyrus Gordon was in attendance, and the famous face of reality television was being led through the murmuring crowd.

'Nice to meet you.' He pushed his hair from his eyes. 'Yes, hello.' He shook a hand. His resplendent tweed jacket of purple hue was outdone only by his custard tie.

A dozen knives and forks of unsuspecting guests hovered over undercooked eggs. Momentarily breakfast was paused; cooling sausages leaked saturated fat from puncture wounds.

Sir Cyrus Gordon was a powdered wig on the head of a vandal king. Outrageous, out of place, impossible to ignore, he lived his caricature. He asked for champagne 'to temper one's thirst' and a kipper to 'nourish the bones'. A pensioner at table four would later swear that the man had been wearing rouge.

'I'm terribly sorry, sir,' the hotel toady fawned, explaining they were out of bubbly. 'A whisky and soda instead?'

Sir Gordon, magnanimous, said he would. He tucked a napkin into his waistcoat and turned to the view of the archipelago. The clatter of cutlery elsewhere in the room was slow to finally resume.

CXXXXD

Dr Frances Quigg sipped on her tea, trying to make this cup last. It was proving impossible to get more hot water for the pot; the staff only had eyes for the clown. Their deference to the man from television was bad enough in itself, but she riled about being passed over. Where had she seen him? One of those singing contests? Making fun of detestable applicants that lacked self-restraint or good judgement? She didn't know who was worse.

The island was out there somewhere. Dr Quigg put her hand involuntarily to her purse, to Black's letter of which she knew every word.

It was flattery, of course, his acknowledgement of her achievements, but at least he was honest about his intentions, and Frances Quigg admired direct speaking. Lord Black offered her funding—he wanted a legacy. He intended to glorify himself in her successes and obtain a tax write off while he did so. How had Black heard about her research ambitions? Dr Quigg had asked herself. There were those who were uncomfortable with her methods, and few, even at the university, knew everything about her plans. He must have done his homework on her, and she found something satisfying in that.

Lord Black offered her the flexibility that private funding would allow. There was no doubt he possessed the resources—Dr Quigg had looked into that. He was money, generational wealth; the family title had been bought in the Industrial Revolution, their largesse knitted in Lancashire looms, influence won in miles of cloth that sold throughout the world. The Blacks had bought companies across the British Empire with the profit from cheap cotton—a slave crop spun into gold. They paid for their society wives out of the toil of the factory floor and collected trinkets with the spoils, the island one of those. And now Lord Black wanted to give his money away and was looking for a worthy cause. The paternal benefactor washing his name as mortality ate at him, no doubt.

Dr Frances Quigg, sixty-five next year, childless, never married. She had always fought and she wasn't used to losing; she would get every penny Black was dangling. Her research institute would one day make history, and there would only be one name on its doors; hers. It was out there, the island, close to the horizon—the key to everything she wanted.

Frances lifted the teapot lid and rattled the hollow china. The waiter, with one drink on his tray, ignored her and walked straight past.

Andrew Sterling remembered the words in the letter: *The Selkie will pick you up.* Wasn't that some sort of mermaid creature, a made-up creature from stories? A sea-lion or seal that turned into a woman to lure sailors onto the rocks? *Daft name for a boat.* Andrew walked from the bus station, carrying his bag and briefcase down to the dock. There were a few boats tied up, but none of them the *Selkie*, and there was no one obvious to ask; nothing around at all but a life-buoy on a weathered pole and a beacon and fog horn at the mouth of the harbour where a couple of kids dangled rods. Andrew checked the time on his phone—still early. He tried to calm himself down.

Why had he destroyed the letter? Because he was smart, of course. No evidence, nothing to trace him; he had been ahead of it from the start. Yet there was an itch to his fingers—Andrew was aware—he would have liked to have held it again. He would open the envelope and read again those words he had memorized. *This is the last, Sterling. The last. You understand?* As if Lord Black were the one making decisions. *I won't give you what you want—no—I won't do that, but this is what I am willing to do.*

Andrew remembered how his own face had blushed reading that for the first time. Who was Black to give orders? But he'd read on.

Instead I will give you twice what you want, twice what you are asking! Think on that! But this is the last time. The words had been underscored twice. *And there is a condition—you will give me the originals. The originals, or you get nothing. I want everything that you have.* Lord Black was making demands. *If you were an honourable man, Mr Sterling, I'd ask you not to make copies or scans, but we both know the sort of person you are.*

Cheeky bugger, being rude like that.

So let me tell you what will happen instead. Deliver the originals and I'll give you double, and that will be the end of all this! You will not contact me again. We will cease to know each other! Far too many exclamation marks. *You will go happily on your way, and if at any future date copies or pictures arise, I will rebuke you and deny them as fakes, and I will pursue you with every lawyer I can buy. I will grind you down, fishmeal man. I will grind you down, and you should know it. Double now and we are through. It is that, or you get nothing.*

Fishmeal. Bloody strange thing to say. Did he mean that as a threat?

Andrew prided himself that he wasn't totally stupid, and so he couldn't help but be annoyed. It was clearly worth a lot to Black if he was willing to pay double now. Why hadn't he asked for more earlier? He cursed himself. Double! He hadn't thought. It was a risk, it had always been a risk, but double would see him good. Not to worry. His lottery ticket had come up this time, and soon he'd be living in style. Andrew hefted his sports bag, weighing the handles, and wondered how much heavier all that money would be and whether he could fit it all in. What would it look like all piled up if he had it in bundles of twenties? Who was kidding who—he was still in the driver's seat, whatever Black might say.

Usual place, usual way, he'd written, the message in the shared email account he had created two years before.

No was the unexpected reply. *I am busy and engaged. If you want it, you will come to the island. You get there from Ellenabeich, near Oban. Look it up. The* Selkie *will be there for you. She sails at 3pm on August 6th. If you want it, don't be late.*

Did Lord Black think he was stupid? Did he think that he, Sterling, would leave the anonymity of London for the solitude of a Scottish rock? Show himself in the middle of nowhere with a copy of the *Telegraph* and a smile? Did Black want him to paint a sign on his back too? *Come and get me. Do me over.* The old fool had no idea.

Andrew heard it before he saw her—the boat approaching the harbour. The *Selkie* was a fair bit bigger than Andrew had expected, but he wasn't sorry for that—the waves were larger down here by the water than they had looked coming up on the coach. She was a low sort of fishing boat with a wide working deck that might stack crab pots, he supposed, though there was nothing of that sort today. Andrew didn't know what he'd been expecting, but this certainly wasn't it; the *Selkie* reminded him of a tug. There were only two men aboard her as far as he could see. One, with a bushy white beard, a poster for fish fingers and granddads everywhere, turned a wheel and brought her close. A second bloke in yellow wellies got up on the rails and held a rope.

Andrew moved down the sloped mooring path that sheltered behind the quay wall. The stone was damp below the last tide line, and his running shoes felt slick. He had brought his bags as he scurried to help, and he now put them down in the way. The wellies man stepped ashore.

'Ahoy!' cried Andrew. The engine was put in reverse and gunned heavily to keep her tight to the harbour wall. Waves slapped. 'Do you need a hand?'

'No, you're good,' said the wellies man. He was in his fifties and Scottish. The fishing boat's engine was cut.

'Andrew Sterling.' Andrew offered and shook the fellow's hand. He sensed the man was uncomfortable.

'Mr MacGregor at your service, sir.' His Highlander's accent was heavy and slow, as if words to be aired should be heard. 'I'm his Lordship's gillie—the gamekeeper. I know your name; you're on the list. Might I ask if the others are with you?'

'The others?' Sterling was annoyed and then annoyed again that he had shown the fellow his surprise.

'All the names on his Lordship's list. The boat only goes once, and we can't wait long. The tide runs strong later on.'

Sterling turned this over in his mind. It made sense of a sort, he supposed. No, he quickly decided, this could be even better—this would definitely work out! The island was not where a man like Lord Black lived the whole year round. Of course not. Black was a man of the world, with business interests; he kept the house and the island for sport. Naturally there should be others along. Likely he would be having guests over for a week to go hunting or play golf—whatever *that* sort did on their private estates while everyone else just got by—orgies and vomitoriums or roasting peasants by the fire. Cigars for the ladies, walks for the men around the billiard table after a gruelling day blasting shot, and too many drinks for all. His own invitation would seem all the more natural amongst a group on a social meeting. No suspicions aroused. And who knew? After his business with Black was complete, perhaps Andrew would stay on for a day or two, just to show there were no bad feelings. Bag a stag, drink the man's brandy. Now that he thought of it, why not? Very soon he would be a person of influence. Andrew Sterling was moving up.

Chapter 2
Troubled Waters

'END OF THE LINE, SIR.'

'This is Oban?'

'Just as she was yesterday and same as she'll be tomorrow.'

Charlie Fotheringham stepped off the train and had a look around. The town hung down on a slope off the hill and crowded about the water. What was it the letter had said? *A car will be there for you to take you to the boat.* Charlie walked the length of the platform towards the exit sign. There was one taxi, in front of which a bellied driver in a v-neck sweater was holding a hand drawn sign. *Black.*

'I think that car is for me,' said a voice in his ear. Charlie nearly jumped. He hadn't heard the man, the large fellow from the train, following a few feet behind. He was older than he'd looked from afar, wrinkled by the sun but still powerful across the shoulders. Formidable was the word.

'Perhaps it's for both of us?' Charlie suggested, recovering. He extended a hand. 'Charlie Fotheringham. Are you going for the boat too? I'm...a guest...of Lord Black.'

'Fotheringham, eh?' The large man eyed Charlie over before conceding a shake of the hand. 'Henry Vail. Pleased to meet you. Do you know if there is anyone else?'

The driver was expecting only two, and they both sat in

the back. Charlie gave his fingers a rub, still aching from the man's grip.

CRXXXD

Henry Vail did not say much. The letter had been clear on some points and very vague on others. He had been surprised to get it; usually any contact from Black had been made indirectly through the company. Of course, Black *was* the company, it wasn't that; but he had never been so personal.

My dear Inspector Vail, I am having a week for a few special friends, those who have done myself and my family great service. I would be very pleased if you would join us, Henry. Naturally, your time will be rewarded. He had signed it AB—Alexander Black—and enclosed a first class ticket on Emirates and wired expenses to his private account. *I will expect you off the Glasgow train, and will have a car waiting for you. Let me know if you are driving instead, so arrangements can be adjusted accordingly.*

Inspector Vail sat back in the car and thought of what was wrong. Black had never called him Henry, never—but then their work had always required a distance. Perhaps, now, in Black's twilight years, the old soak was getting soft? Henry bit his nail, a habit only when something bothered him. Why bring him all the way to the island? Their relationship was one of cash. Inspector Vail fidgeted with his coat and balled his hand into a wide fist.

Something else bothered him too. This Charlie figure, sharing the car—what was going on there? Black was in his sixties, and this kid was half that age. No wedding ring. No girlfriend with him. What sort of a guest was he?

CRXXXD

Something is worrying him, thought Charlie, squeezed. There was scarcely any room in the back of the car, and Mr Vail barely fit in. He was a friend of Lord Black's, that's what he'd said, and had flown in for the week from Asia. Charlie had noticed the bag as the driver had loaded their luggage.

The high street was shared by tourist coaches, tradesmen's vans, and tightly parked cars. A row of small shops lined one side of the front street, more than one tartan shop up For Let. Sandstone walls and storm-proof glass told that summer was only fleeting, the pavement drying off between showers. The car nudged forward another fifty yards until they got stuck at another light.

'That's a curious thing. What is it?' Charlie asked the driver as the town leered up on his left. Oban was stacked like a steep amphitheatre around the stage that was her small port, and above the balconies of the highest houses a coliseum sat as her crown.

'McCaig's Folly,' explained the local of the pint-sized gladiatorial arena. 'Built a hundred years ago after something he saw in Rome. Too much money on his hands. I bet he never had to drive for a living.'

But it was gone. The road wound to gain some height, and just like that they were out in fields. They had left the little town in their rear view mirror and set off along the coast.

The car headed south along a thin strip of road that, eight miles out, became narrower still as they turned off to a road on the right. Soon they were dipping and diving through countryside at a tremendous turn of speed.

An inane torrent of cheerful chatter spewed from the radio. 'And what can we expect this weekend, Moira?' Moira predicted fair weather. Charlie thought about mentioning the army to Vail, but he was not of that man's generation. Whatever it was that Vail had done, the Falklands perhaps, he hadn't done it in a George Bush war.

Charlie caught glimpses of well-fed sheep through the limbs of bunkered trees. 'Is this a one way road?' he asked hopefully, concerned about their speed, given the absence of lanes. The driver threw on the brakes and ducked into a lay-by to avoid a head-on collision with a bus. Charlie felt his stomach move, his question answered. 'How far do we have to go?'

⊙⊗⊗⊙

Sir Cyrus Gordon never travelled alone, and on this trip he had brought a relative, distant though it was. The Rhesus macaque monkey was the size of a well-fed house cat, its curling tail full twice its length and crisp white like its needle-tooth smile. Cyrus fed scraps to the beast through the cage, strips of smoked fish he'd brought back from breakfast, which he passed through the bars to be plucked immediately and devoured with a ravished haste. *Chatter, chatter, chatter* went the sharp little teeth; somehow the animal missed his fingers but got every scrap. 'Hungry little blighter. Look at you!; Cyrus shook the cage and set the creature howling. It jumped across the bars. Cyrus bared his teeth and growled at it, which stirred the animal more. The Rhesus showed its fangs; it hopped and howled.

'Is he all right, sir?' The commotion had drawn the maid who was tidying up the room.

'What's it to you? Don't you have something to do? Just hurry up and pack everything away!' There were four of five suitcases around, the clothes turned out of them all. Cyrus poured himself a drink from the decanter and put his feet up on the bed. The French doors to the small balcony off his room were open and let in the air. Cyrus looked at the woman's arse as she bent over to pick up his scattered things. He swirled the whisky around his mouth, stirring it with his tongue.

'Don't you complain, Ming,' he chastised the monkey. 'There are children dying of hunger every day while you gorge yourself and play.'

He could hear the sea. Over the dragging of cases and the occasional squawk, he heard the ocean break near. The persistence. The repetitive on and on and on of the surf taking a run at the shore. His view, beyond his poky room, afforded him a slice of the mainland as it fell down and gave way to the Atlantic. *Here the ocean has won,* he thought. *Beyond here man has no claim.*

He poured another drink. The bottle was near empty; it was time to be making that boat. Time to go see what his friend was up to with his letter and vague promises of fun. What was it that Blackie had said? *A week of frolics and debauchery, and no one to tell a soul.* Sir Cyrus liked the sound of that. He hadn't seen Alex in quite a while; you were never as close as you were in school. The bastard always had gobs of money from that rich family of his, but now Cyrus was the successful one. Now Cyrus was the Lord! The public as entertainment—priceless. They couldn't get enough of him.

'Go and get help,' he addressed the maid. 'I need all my things brought down. Have someone take them over to the harbour, pronto, and be careful of Emperor Ming!'

'Yes, sir. At once. Of course.'

The way she looked at him, Cyrus knew he could have her if he wanted. It was a burden, all this fame, money, and good looks. Cyrus finished his glass and burst out laughing. The monkey soon joined in.

Dr Frances Quigg settled her bill, keeping the receipt for expenses. There was no one on hand to assist her with her bag, and so she rolled it herself down to the harbour. She had to stand aside as a Range Rover plied past her, filling all of the road. She muddied her shoes as there was no pavement to save her, much to her annoyance.

At the pier a crowd had gathered, half on and half off a stout boat. They all seemed to be waiting for something; perhaps the man in the wellies waving his arms? The car that had forced her off the road was stuck trying to turn around. *Serves them right,* thought Dr Quigg. *I hope they are stuck there forever.*

A sloping path ran to the tide behind the great stones of the harbour wall, where a handful of paint-worn fishing boats huddled behind its arm.

'Are you with the party, ma'am?' asked welly boots man, a civil fellow with a beard; Scottish stock.

'I am Doctor Quigg,' answered Frances primly, and waited while he ticked off a clipboard.

'Mr MacGregor, ma'am, at your service. I'll get your bag on board. Have a seat, please, if you will,' he said as he extended his hand and helped her.

A young man already on the boat—he could be scarcely out of college—passed his hand through his overgrown hair. *Zit-ridden oaf* was Quigg's assessment after he failed to give up his seat. Two other men remained on the quay, hesitant to board. The young handsome one was talking on his mobile phone, pacing back and forth. He had spectacles of the old-fashioned sort that Dr Quigg associated with black and white movies. She liked him, whoever he was. The camel coat man had a face like his hands, square and rough and hard. He didn't pace; he stood and observed. Dr Quigg could not keep his eye.

'Is this the only boat to Mr Black's island, or is there a regular ferry?' she asked the welly boot.

'There's no public boat to Lord Black's island. He chartered this 'specially for you all.'

'And how long does it take? How long is the crossing?'

'She's no that far, ma'am, but we'll take it easy. You'll be there in under half an hour.'

Dr Quigg recalled the slate-grey sea and the flicker of light from the wave caps. The shadow that rose to fill the sky looked further away than that, but maybe it was an illusion? Perhaps Black's island and all her funding was closer to civilization than it looked.

'My goodness. What's this coming now?' Welly boots looked concerned. Quigg scrunched her face in agitation; it was unmistakable and annoying.

CXXXXD

'Make way for the Emperor. You, sonny, you'll have to move. Ming always sits in the back.' Sir Cyrus displaced the drape-haired boy and had the hotel staff load in his things. He took a couple of coins from his pocket and didn't notice the disappointed looks. 'Gordon,' he stuck out his hand to the old tart in greeting, but the grey-bun didn't shake. 'Pleased to meet you,' he said to her anyway.

'We've already met, Mr Gordon.'

She was someone's grandmother, that was it, but for the life of him he couldn't remember. 'Well, splendid to see you again.'

And as for the rest of them, the new kitchen help, they should be underdeck or kept out of sight. Old Blackie should really have the staff taken over in a separate run.

There was a couple of muscle, father and son, probably there to keep DB safe; yes, there was no mistaking Big Pockets himself, Douglas Bowers the Trois in the flesh.

'DB! Cyrus Gordon! Here for the shooting?' He pumped his arm and slapped his shoulder like old times. And who was this, his tasty friend? Who was this treat coiled up in the corner?

'My assistant, Ms Hedringer,' DB introduced.

'Joan.' She shook. Cyrus had a thing for leather gloves. 'Did your parcel just make a noise, Mr Gordon?'

'Ignore him, please. He doesn't like water. Ming's more fun when he's on dry land.'

'What the hell are we waiting for? The large American gentleman in the white suit barked the question to everyone.

'There is still one on the list to come, sir.' The gillie, MacGregor, had a face of weathered stone that didn't wholly mask his agitation.

'There ain't any room for a damn 'nother soul. How many were you thinking of taking?'

Indeed, to Mr MacGregor's eye, the objection appeared

quite sound. There was a great deal of luggage, far more than he had expected, and he wasn't sure there were life-jackets for them all. MacGregor looked to catch the captain's eye, but the skipper of the *Selkie* seemed unconcerned.

'Might I remind you again, sir, that the lady with you is *not* on the list, and by rights she should not be coming.' MacGregor looked at the woman one more time and then down at the name he had added. Joan Hedringer. He had crossed it out once and re-written it once more, having to make her spell it. Why did he feel himself blush? There was no escaping she was a handsome woman, modestly dressed and well turned out. She sat at the back, her legs crossed and pulled beneath her, her sheer nylons tight over her calves. *Well*, thought MacGregor, *it's no business of mine—I'm a gamekeeper, not a doorman.*

'She's my goddamn nurse, just as I told you, and she's stayin', do you hear? You going to answer to your boss if I keel over?'

Mr MacGregor was not entirely sure how his employer would respond to the suggestion. Not having actually met Lord Black yet, he was at a disadvantage to say. Mr MacGregor did not reveal this fact to Mr Bowers, but even if he had, it is unlikely that this peculiarity—one amongst the many surrounding the strangers on the boat—would have influenced the events that followed. Or maybe it would have changed everything.

In any event, Mr MacGregor said instead, 'We are still short the company of a Miss Eleanor Grace. I have my orders to give her until three fifteen, and leave her if she's a minute beyond that.'

But at that moment on the pier a chauffeur-driven Bentley pulled up. Mr MacGregor's list was complete, plus one additional passenger.

The mainland dropped behind the *Selkie* and they cut dark water all around. In the clear light of a summer after-noon, a distant island grew large.

CXXXD

Andrew Sterling raised himself for the view, one hand on the side of the cabin, one foot up on the rail. They had crossed the channel, a short sea, and before them surf broke into spray.

'Many a boat has wound up sorry when its crew were looking beyond,' MacGregor let him know. Andrew could see why. Trailings of rock stood half submerged, tread marks left behind by the ice age. Most of these outcrops were in bits and pieces, the preserve of birds or sea-lions. The chain of low rock, bleached at the tide line, rose a few wind-worn feet from the wet.

'These were a ship's ruin, back in the day,' MacGregor narrated. The gillie stood back and to the side of the wheel-house with a good view over the deck. 'They've gone and automated the lighthouses around here.'

Andrew could make it out now that it was pointed out to him—a forlorn lookout on the tip of the nearest spear, blinking even though it was daylight. How they had managed to build it out here was beyond the powers of his imagination, but Andrew wasn't interested in lighthouses. Beyond these dangers rose the island proper, showing the broken side of her face. In less than an hour he would be on shore and looking Lord Black in the face. And then the fun would begin.

CXXXD

What had Charlie been expecting? Some volcanic plinth of lava stone rising out of a coral sea? It looked worn down, scrubbed down, like a defeated heap. He found himself a little disappointed. The spray had left drops of water on his glasses, and he took them off and wiped them clear. It had but the one mountain, the island in front of them, and even that slid off, fallen into the sea as if hewn by an enormous blade. *Quite the cliffs on that side,* he supposed. *Think of the bloody wind.* The island. Black's island, here on the edge of the world. Next stop, Greenland or New York. It was the very definition of remote.

'Is that it?' Charlie Fotheringham asked needlessly.

'Aye,' confirmed MacGregor. 'That's where his Lordship's at. That's his island there.'

'And the castle...the house...what's it called?'

'Taigh Dubh. Black house, it means.'

'Tie dye?'

'Taigh Dubh,' MacGregor repeated patiently.

'Tie do? Tie Do!'

'Close enough, sir. You'll be trying to spell the thing next.'

⊂⊗⊗⊃

Magnificent. Dr Frances Quigg assessed the growing view. Whatever cataclysm on that extraordinary day had sheared the island's mountain had left behind it a sea-bird sanctuary that sheltered thousands of feathered creatures. A dozen species nested on its cliffs and fed from the herring-rich waters beneath. Black wing-tipped gannet, kittiwake, and the long-billed cormorant she'd seen without her glasses. Skullcapped tern and penguin-looking guillemot she knew were resident also. And puffins. Puffins too. Who didn't like a puffin?

'The Vikings saw this very view. They called that mountain Odin's Anvil, though I don't know how you say it in Norse. They sailed through here from Scandinavia to Ireland, en route to the Isle of Man,' she said, although to no one in particular.

'Good times, good times,' Cyrus Gordon answered. 'Makes you sad you were born when there was penicillin.'

How like that sneering boor from the hotel to make light of the things that matter.

'The early abbey on the island of Iona is only a few miles off.'

'Can you see it?' Cyrus asked.

'No. Maybe from the mountain. Perhaps we'll get the chance to climb and look.'

'You go right ahead, dear.'

Don't you 'dear' me, you speckled peacock. Who do you think you are?

'They started work on the Book of Kells there, you know. It's a thing called a *Bible*—introduced a thing called *Christianity.*'

'Did they now? Very interesting. And how did your Vikings take to that place while they were holidaying through these waters?'

'Plundered it mercilessly. Killed the monks.'

'Oh, dear. Sorry to hear it. Good times, good times. Like I said.'

⬡⬡⬡⬡⬡

'There's nothing else near. How's he get his groceries then?' Andrew Sterling was asking MacGregor.

'You're standing on it,' answered the Scot.

'And he comes all the way out here to hang out at that place? It's out in the middle of nowhere.'

'Perhaps,' MacGregor suggested diplomatically, 'that's the very point.'

⬡⬡⬡⬡⬡

Strange land, thought Douglas Bowers III who had dined with five American presidents. *Not like what you get back home.*

He looked at the island drawing closer, and it was the same as the road from the helicopter. Scrub that they called heather and tough grasses that liked to clump and everywhere, everywhere, wherever you looked, a few of those God-damned sheep. But it wasn't all that which was different from home, it was the trees, he finally figured out. Or more correctly, the absence of trees. Whether he was in his ranch up in the Blue Mountains or hunting in Colorado, the landscape was one of forest. Sure they had mountains, rivers, and streams bigger than those around here. Sure they did. But whether you were in the redwoods of Northern California or up in the Rocky Mountains, the place was a land of wood. But not here. *Why not?* he wondered. It wasn't Nebraska; they weren't farming it. *You're not in Kansas anymore.* Nearly all of the trees here had gone, and the ones that were left were wizened and twisted, bent old women against the wind. Surely there had been trees here sometime, where there was now rocks and grass and that heather. Someone had come in the night and plucked them out, like a witch stealing kids from their bedroom.

Eleanor Grace reclined on the box that MacGregor had told them contained a life raft in the unlikely event one was needed. Wind off the sea threw her hair about wildly, but she didn't mind. She closed her eyes and drew her coat snug, finding the sun by its feel on her face. Below her was the deep blue sea and above her the endless sky. *Horizon,* she thought. *We live on the horizon. We live on the razor's edge.* The slice of noise that was other people. Below her, a mile deep? Two miles? Three? With water you could never tell. What was important was the sense of infinity that stretched beneath her and above her as well. *Twinkle, twinkle,* she thought. One star, one little star, warming the front of her eyelids, all the countless billion others hidden by its glow. Mile upon mile of vacuum and dust. Nobody knew what was out there. A little sliver, a veneer of flesh was all there was between the deep beneath her and the everything that existed above. Eleanor floated, suspended between, on her horizon at latitude zero. She pulsed with life and was so happy that she thought she might fade away. As it happened, it was the sound of alien chattering, a howling screech, that brought her around. Eleanor opened a curious eye. Whatever had made the sound wasn't human.

'Careful of your fingers.'

Henry Vail, hand outstretched, pulled his arm back from the package. The parcel looked like it might hold a birdcage, and something inside it was alive. The *Selkie* rose and fell on the swell, and whatever was in the cage was agitated.

'You can take the beast out of the savage jungle, but not the savage out of the beast!' Sir Cyrus clearly enjoyed this little speech, which Vail suspected was often repeated. He was not certain the phrasing was logically watertight but had doubt enough to hold his own tongue.

'This is my Emperor Ming. Say hello to the nice man, Ming!' Cyrus pulled back the covers. The occupant was not a feathered friend; the occupant was far more mammalian. 'He'd like to sink those choppers into you!' Gordon enthused. 'Give him half a chance and he will. I've seen him take lumps out of people.' He seemed to take great pleasure in the memory.

Vail had the urge to punch the man; the beast had given him a bit of a shock. The animal, divested of the security behind its blanket, barked and shrieked without pause. Inspector Henry Vail had seen monkeys before—in Asia there were plenty of temples that were crawling with the buggers. They were thieves, sly, and beggars for food; they would go for your sunglasses or an earring. The stupid tourists kept feeding the things, and the locals thought it unlucky to chase them. Bloody pests. Carried disease. Vail had no love for pets, though he did admire a cunning intelligence. That monkey looked at you smart. Henry Vail kept his fingers away.

Eleanor Grace watched the drama, waiting for her line. 'Might we ask why you brought her with you?' she asked its owner. 'Have you scared off the rest of the debutantes?' She was wrapped from knee to collar in faux Arctic fox, over-done if it weren't for the wind.

'I make a habit of going to the movies,' Gordon began. 'I've seen a bit of you up on the screen.'

'Just a bit?' She left her lips open. Her agent had told her this made her look coy. Lipstick smeared on her rolled ciga-rette. Strings of her hair fluttered, untamed.

'You were an Egyptian Queen,' Gordon continued.

'They didn't wear much back in those days.' Eleanor Grace blinked at him through heavily kohled eyes. She was the only one, besides the monkey perhaps, who wasn't somewhat chilled.

'No indeed. It looked very hot. All that sand, I suppose.'

Ming gave a series of howls, and Gordon dropped the sheet.

'Adorable,' said Miss Grace, extending her cigarette for Sir what's-his-name to light.

'And you are staying all week?' he asked her, doing the honours.

'I am now.' She inhaled.

⟨⊗⊗⟩

Andrew Sterling tried to act naturally. He struggled to zip up a bomber jacket that was the warmest thing he had brought. His coming here was meant to be a secret, and now he was trying to rationalize the fact that he recognized three people on this boat.

Andrew basked in the glow of second-hand radiation that is thrown by the presence of celebrity. *That's Sir Cy! No doubt about it. Will it be okay if I tell my mates?* You couldn't go through a supermarket counter in Britain without see-ing a picture of Cyrus Gordon in the racks, whose indiscre-tions and transgressions had been good for miles of print;

the drinking and the clubs; his wife's suicide; the careers he made happen or shot down; the street girl singer from the first show who had ended up with a bun in the oven from our man. That story ran and ran. *What was her name?* Andrew couldn't remember; he'd only watched the first two series. Hanging out with Sir Cy was definitely big league, even if the old boy dyed his hair. But no, he couldn't tell his mates. *Then they'll be asking what I was doing out here, and we can't be having that. No way, no can do. Keep it on the low and narrow. Do the deed and then move on, that's the Andrew motto.*

He knew the old doll in the fur coat, too. *She'd been famous once upon a time.* He remembered his mum was a fan. Or maybe she was one of those model types who were hired to look like Hollywood stars. *She's still got a bit of it going on; I can't say that I'd say no. Note to self; get on YouTube, check what she looked like back when.*

Those two belonged. Andrew could see how that worked—the famous and the moneyed coming together—they fit with his idea of Black. And then the other one. Had he expected to see that face again? He admitted to himself that he had. Better wait until they had privacy to talk, for there was a lot to catch up on. No, it was the rest of the crowd that seemed odd; it was the rest of them he couldn't figure out.

What's the deal with the overweight Yank? He had the look of a cowboy. *I bet he's an oil man,* figured Andrew. *Aberdeen, something in the North Sea over here, the other side of the pond, come to check up on his rigs.*

And the scary looking bloke with the nose? *Definitely hired muscle.* Andrew was wary. *But is he Black's, or someone else's?* Difficult to know right now.

'By the power of Grayskull,' Andrew muttered.

'What was that?' Inspector Henry Vail answered. He'd noticed the kid watching him.

'Nothing, mate, sorry. Clearing my throat.'

There he goes again—can't keep his fingers away. Have a go, mate, give the monkey a rub! Planet of the Apes meets itself. Not sure which one of them should be behind bars. Like looking into a mirror, mate, isn't it? He forgave Cyrus then; the monkey was brilliant! *Go on, give the bastard a bite!*

'What do you do?' The voice came from down near his shoulder.

Andrew was startled. 'Errr...sorry?' he replied. He hadn't noticed the old lady come and sit by him. Face powder rubbed off her chin.

'It's a simple enough question, young man. I know where you are going, obviously, but I don't know why you are here. I wonder if it has something to do with your occupation; so I ask, how do you know Lord Black?'

Andrew had unkind thoughts. *There's a house made of sweeties in the Hansel and Gretel woods going unoccupied this weekend.*

'I'm an actor.' He told the lie he'd prepared earlier. 'I act, that's what I do.'

'An actor that acts. I'm glad you clarified that. And you are here to perform for Lord Black?'

'Nah. Nothing like that, you know. No shows going on. We're acquainted.'

'You're a rent boy, then? You've been hired for sex? Does that sort of thing pay well?'

'What you on about, lady? What you doing saying things like that for? If he could have, Andrew would have moved away.

'We're just getting to know each other, young man. That's all. No need to get testy, I'm sure.'

◌⊗◌

Dr Frances Quigg was making friends. Young Andrew Sterling—she had introduced herself—had a ruffled look that might pass for handsome these days amongst girls of undeveloped minds. She was pretty sure he was a liar. What sort of actor didn't brush his teeth? Even the ugly ones were narcissists. No, there was a mystery to Mr Sterling; he wasn't an actor at all, but what he was, she didn't care. She was sure he had no claim on Lord Black's money, and she wasn't interested in anything else.

∞⊗∞

'It was Mr MacGregor, you said?' Charlie sheltered near the wheelhouse, pleased to be out of the wind.

'That's right, sir.'

'My name's Fotheringham.'

'I remember, sir.'

'You can call me Charlie if you like.'

MacGregor didn't call him anything at all.

It looked further than it was, yet closer than it would have if the weather had been worse.

'Is that it?'

'Aye, you get a glimpse of the house once we round the headland. Up here the currents run strong. It was choppy coming over, sir. Best to hold onto something.'

Mr MacGregor had scarcely finished the words before the boat slipped side on to a wave, and the *Selkie* listed something awful. There was an elbow raised and much flailing of arms, and at the same time a crash and a spill. Who went clattering into whom was not immediately obvious. People clutched at poles and seats and held onto whatever they could. The passengers, those few not pressed back on the benches, staggered as the *Selkie* rode through the crest. Mr Sterling was thrown to the deck and thought he had broken his arse. Baggage rolled around. The monkey's cage sprang loose.

'Ming!' Sir Cyrus lurched for the cage, his grasping hand almost touching it—almost, but not close enough. Overboard it went. The cage seemed to float, howling for a moment, before it vanished like a cheap magician's trick. The blanket flattened, a black square on a gun-metal sea. Emperor Ming had gone.

The boat drifted on. There was nothing that any of

them could do to help, and a shocked silence settled over the guests as the *Selkie* turned her nose into the waves. Their pilot had dimmed the engines during the commotion, but now he lit them up again. 'Unlucky to bring beasts on board.' It was the first thing the captain had said.

Chapter 3
The Letter

'Do they get wifi? I'm not picking anything up.'

'Help me with this, be so good.'

The *Selkie* lingered only long enough to see its passengers put to shore. Suitcases, hatboxes, and wheelie cases were ferried across her gunnel to the pier. Mr MacGregor heaved, and Charlie Fotheringham stood forward on shore to help with the clearing of the deck.

'You're staying with us, Mr. MacGregor?' he asked as the Scotsman pushed the boat off.

'I'm to look after you all this week long. I'm not to no give you a hand.'

Charlie was left on the jetty to fathom the inscrutability of the offer, as the others had already moved down the path. He raised a hand in farewell to the *Selkie* and felt foolish when it was not returned.

❦

The approach to the house renewed Dr Quigg, who was awash with quiet excitement. She had a number of venial sins chalked up against her, and Pride was a regular visitor. Lord Black she had fancied as being an extravagant man, and here was the evidence before her, in stone and mortar, to prove how astute she was.

Taigh Dubh was fully a hundred yards to a side and laid out like a martial fort. Its red granite stone walls to its crenelated battlements stood ready to repel attack. Castle turrets rose above the roofline, each guarding one corner of the house. The archers would have a fine view to the enemy arrayed with its pennants below. Yet it was all for show. All entertainment. Endless money in pursuit of fashion. There were no arrow slits or murder holes hiding guards with boiling oil. No threat in earnest. None apparent. Nothing but aesthetics to defend. No, no, Dr Quigg mulled, none of that and the better for it; the entire castle was straight from a play. Glazed windows cut holes in this faux fortress, good for light but bad at keeping out raiders streaming up from the sea. No armies would array on its croquet lawns or launch catapults to clear the topiary. Taigh Dubh's perimeter was ringed by no moat or barbican of piled earth; the house was armoured in glass canopies and greaved in marble steps.

'Have you been to Taigh Dubh before, Madam?' the weathered gillie asked at her side. MacGregor carried her bags, leaving those of the other guests back at the jetty, promising to return with the tractor.

'No, this is my first visit,' answered Dr Quigg.

'Well, I hope you find the lodge in order. It's quite a splendid home.'

Dr Quigg tried to tally the sum. Two stories tall and dozens of rooMs How much were those mill workers paid? What did it matter? They were long gone. How much did Lord Black have in his pockets for her? Her quiet excitement returned.

◌⬗⬖◌

'I'm sorry, I didn't get your name.'

'Hedringer. Joan Hedringer. Pleased to meet you, Mr... Fotheringhill?'

'Fotheringham. Charles. Call me Charlie. Everybody does.' He lifted his hat and laughed.

'Well, Charlie, if you insist. But then you must call me Joan. Don't mind DB too much. He's like that with nearly everyone.'

It had crossed Charlie's mind a couple of times—who were all these people with him? People that Lord Black knew, of course, but were they the sort of people that should be in his biography? What had they to do with the man?

'I must say, Joan, you took that very well. I thought you might find it all terribly embarrassing. An awful spot for that man to put you in.' He felt an affinity for Ms Hedringer. She, like himself, was an outsider.

'Oh, you mean back there?' Joan gave him a look, but thought his sympathies well meant. 'DB is so used to getting his way, he sometimes overlooks the details.'

MacGregor had been polite enough, but he had still tried to turn her away. Charlie had felt rotten for both of them and cringed to think of it again. It didn't seem to faze Ms Hedringer, however—what fortitude she must possess! Until then he had been friendless, an impostor, out of sorts amidst the select crowd at the pier, but Ms Hedringer's situation had given him courage and settled him down. He'd found a friend without knowing her name—Joan. It suited her well. Charlie became very self-conscious of how close she was beside him. He caught himself stealing glances at her under pretence of examining the view. His mind was stamped by little details that were defining Ms Hedringer for him; her straight black hair in a pony tail, held off her face by a silver clasp that looked like a leaf of some sort, the pronounced curve at the top of her lip that made him think of a cat's smile, her habit of glancing at him from the corner of her eye before turning her head when she talked, and the v-notch of elastic at the top of her boot that almost hid a muscular calf.

'All the same, I thought you took it very well,' he repeated. 'Shows a strength of character.'

'Thank you, Charlie. Aren't you kind? But you don't get to work for a man like Mr Bowers by being a delicate flower.'

'I imagine you get resolute, dealing with patients' ailments.'

She didn't answer straight away. 'Something like that, yes.'

What had been natural now felt uncomfortable. What was it she didn't want to say? They walked side by side across the rolled trim lawns that swept like a carpet to the house. Up a gentle slope stood Taigh Dubh, surrounded by gardens and low walls.

'That's quite the thing.'

'Lovely, isn't it?'

'Good lord, is that a golf course too?' At the edge of the bay stood a sentinel tee box, and a distant pennant snapped over a green.

'I suppose I'll find out now if Mr MacGregor was right. Will Lord Black let me in, do you think?'

She was smiling. Putting on a good show, thought Charlie. Rotten of Bowers to make her uncomfortable. Dreadful manners of the Yank.

Joan continued, 'Do you think they'll raise the drawbridge before I get inside, or will they wait to turn me out?'

'I'm sure it was just an oversight to leave you off the list. Lord Black owes you an apology.'

'Much more likely Mr Bowers didn't let him know. I was a late addition.'

'Well, I'm certain Lord Black will be very understanding, Charlie laughed. But in the event this proved far from the truth.

⊗⊗⊗⊗⊗

'Yes, sir, this way, please.' MacGregor showed him in.

DB liked what he saw. It reminded him of Hearst in San Simeon back Stateside, which he'd visited a few times in California—the inspiration for *Citizen Kane,* they said. Left his mark on the world, did Hearst. Who would know him now if it weren't for that? Something of quality out of the wild. Who today remembered his detractors? *Something that lasts in this world, that's what counts, the rest of it is snow in the springtime.* Places like this took decades to build; why not buy the entire thing wholesale and save time? The whole island, mountains, animals and all! He could have it all and put his name on the door. The only people living on the island were folks who worked for Lord Black—he'd checked it out—employees, every last one. He could turn this into whatever he pleased, and the workmanship was second to none. Christ, he'd imagined falling turrets and damp dungeons; he'd pictured a pile of money to fix the place up. He hadn't reckoned it would be in such good taste. A few updates and he could move right in. These people only stayed here a few weeks each year! Why, not only that, there was enough flat land—he could bulldoze that golf course—and it would take an airstrip with no effort at all. Sure, he'd have to talk to London about those flight rules, but that would only be a matter of time. Governments wanted favourable PR, every one of them the same. What was the point of owning a few newspapers if you couldn't scratch a back from time to time? Quid pro quo. Lend a hand. *Oh, yes,* thought DB, rubbing his hands, *there could be some rare times to be had here.* Even Margo couldn't disapprove. Margo would like the gardens.

'Hey, Mac,' he called out to the burdened gillie, the man's hands full of luggage and such. 'Send over someone to fetch me a drink. Could you manage that when you have a minute?'

MacGregor paused before attempting the stairs. 'If sir would like, there's a cabinet in the drawing room here or a tray in the billiard room off of the corridor.'

'I gotta get my own drink? Isn't there a housekeeper? Where's the rest of the staff around this place? Don't you have caterers or something for us?'

MacGregor teetered on the second stair. 'Just myself and

Mrs MacGregor, sir, but if you'll excuse me for the present.'

'Are you kidding me? You and your wife are running this place?'

'There was a gardener, sir, but he's done for the season.'

DB's eyes lit up; his mouth felt dry. 'Where was that tray you were mentioning?'

'In the billiard room, sir, off of the corridor. It's not a full-size table. There's snooker too, and a set of pool balls for anyone that wants them. Will that be everything for now?'

DB found it. He poured himself a great big scotch out of the oldest, most expensive-looking bottle. He looked around for ice, but finding none he settled on a splash of soda. Lord Black must be really scraping the barrel if he could only afford that old pair. DB figured the asking price, which was as steep as they came, was asking for a hammer and chisel. The thought made him even happier.

⟨⊗⊗⊗⟩

'Yours was once her Ladyship's rooms, ma'am,' explained the housekeeper as she escorted Eleanor.

Mrs MacGregor was as short as her husband was long and there was hardly any meat on her. Tight dark hair pulled back in a bun was strung through with gray and silver. Wiry was the word. She looked used to hard work.

'Her Ladyship isn't staying here now?'

'I was meaning Mrs Monica, ma'am. His present Lordship's grandmother.'

'You're putting me in the granny suite? Forgive me if I don't sound excited.'

'Oh, no, ma'am. Nothing like that. It's the finest suite we have.'

They were upstairs on the southern wing, walking towards the corner.

'Who's got a bigger room than I? And don't give me any half answers.'

'None of them, ma'am, I swear! Not a one. Even his

Lordship's is smaller. Lady Monica—you can see her in the pictures—she dressed like the queen she was.'

This mollified Eleanor Grace somewhat. 'It has a view, I trust?'

'The best, ma'am. Yes. His Lordship gave specific instructions: no-one to have this room but you. He made a special point.'

Eleanor quietly purred. His Lordship was a gentleman. It had been a long time since she'd had one of those. 'And where is the present Lady Black these days? Is Lord Black's wife staying up here with him?'

'No, ma'am. His Lordship is only recently married. I'm told her Ladyship is to come on after, but she's in Australia or Canada or somewhere. His Lordship hunts here with his friends. It's a private week, alone.'

'Yes. With his friends.' *Not his lady wife.* 'And tell me'—Eleanor paused for a second, unsure if the housekeeper was a confidant—'do my rooms connect with his Lordship's?'

Oh, no, I'm sure not, ma'am,' the housekeeper's voice hushed. 'You have nothing to worry about there. His Lordship's rooms are at the top of the north tower, on the complete other side of the house.'

The gillie, Mr MacGregor, was sweating when he was done. He'd taken the tractor back for the bags, but had to humph them himself up each stair. Only one small bag left in the entry hall, nearly lost in the shadows under the coats. And no cage to carry up, either.

Charlie opened his leather satchel and laid his notebooks out on the desk. He stacked them to the right of his laptop, which showed 38% battery left. He put his Dictaphone on the right, the old sort with an actual tape. It helped him sort his thoughts out to talk into it when there was a lot going on in his head. The room's windows were imperious, the ceiling eleven or twelve feet tall. *Goodness knows how they heat the place when the winds of winter blow.* He had two journals filled with Lord Black's family history, as much as he'd been able to acquire. It was his habit to handwrite notes and put them into order as he transcribed them onto his computer later; he'd never been able to cultivate the knack of typing his thoughts first time. But that didn't worry him. No. What terrified him was the empty file on the laptop still awaiting his first attempt at the book.

The Biography of Lord Alexander Black
Working title: *The Dark Isle.*

Word count: eleven.

By any definition… thin.

'When can I see Lord Black?' he asked MacGregor's wife.

'His Lordship is out and will be back soon, sir. By dinner, I suppose. Drinks at six. Dinner at eight. Anything sir needs, just ring.' The housekeeper pointed out a braided pull rope dangling by the door to his suite. An old wired telephone sat on a table by the wall, and Charlie asked about it. 'I don't believe that's worked in a while,' he was told. He picked up the handset; it was dead. Charlie checked his own phone—no service, of course, but he saw a network from somebody's iPhone, asking if he wanted to join.

'Is that yours? Has someone else got a connection here?'

'I'm sorry, sir, I can't say either way. Me and my husband don't go for these things. If that's everything, I'll leave you in peace.'

⎯⎯⎯

Inspector Henry Vail took a practical assessment of the quarters where he'd been billeted. One door in, lockable. Henry did so and pocketed the key. Two windows, one seized.

Henry lifted the other one, although the too-judicious use of paint made the job quite difficult. The window was big enough to climb through, and Henry poked his head out for a look. The castle was built around an inner courtyard, where a pond and outdoor furniture were visible. A slate sloped roof ran the circumference whose tiles would be slick in the rain. Henry had checked the BBC on the plane and knew it had been dry last week. An iron drainpipe thirty feet to his left led up the outside of a turret wall. Closer to his right was another drainpipe that fell all the way to the ground. Henry was sure either pipe would bear his weight, but he was less certain of the securing bolts. Every window on the inside wall appeared to be within reach. Every room was visible from half a dozen directions, including his very own. Henry withdrew his head, closing the window. He fished his pockets and brought out a coin, balancing it on the ledge. In the event of disturbance, it was sure to fall off. Henry then closed the curtains too. He turned on the single lamp in the room, which burned with a low-wattage bulb. The light pulsed as the electricity surged and faded, and this struck him as a little strange. He unwrapped the parcel of paper and string, and he dismantled and cleaned the gun.

Cyrus held the Granny Smith out in his open hand, one bite mark short of whole. 'It's your favourite. It's nice and tart. I'll let you have it all.' Emperor Ming did not come for the offering, though apples were his favourite. Sir Cyrus Gordon was patient. 'Not like Black to go all democratic, skimping on the servants and staff,' he said. 'I'll be damned if he thinks I'm pressing my own suits. That housekeeper of his better be good.' It was not apparent to whom he was talking; there was no one in the room but himself, and an answer was not forthcoming.

'Are you listening to me, Ming?' Cyrus cocked an ear for a moment—distant doors banged, that was all, and beyond that there wasn't a sound. Ming, if he was craning an ear from the bottom of the sea, did not deign to reply. Cyrus's eyes tightened and squeezed a tear; his lips pinched, his arms shook. He pitched the apple with a fierce overhead toss, and it shattered as it hit the wall. A small wet mark was left on the paper, the shrapnel scattered amongst his bags. Cyrus ignored this as he took a moment. His jaw gradually unclenched. 'I'm sorry, Ming, that was rude of me. I'll have the housekeeper clean it up.' Yet he felt a little better for all the mess.

Cyrus picked up his wine glass and carried it to the window. There was a garden outside, one of those symmetrical laid-out ones that his own mother had taken such pleasure in. There was a pagoda at its centre, its door turned away. Quite a private spot, he took note. As he mulled over the practicality of a pagoda, a woman emerged on the patio below. She wore a long blue dress, the skirt painted with yellow flowers, and she made her way out into the garden. The woman was covered by a large straw sunhat (quite unnecessarily, Cyrus thought; this was Scotland after all) that left him guessing who it was. *Turn around, you snippet. Let's have a look.* But the woman, whoever she was, did not. Cyrus sipped slowly from his glass. The woman was clearly no servant; she was dressed like a lady and walked with the aimless pace of somebody killing time. She stopped to take the smell of a rose bush. Might it be Eleanor, or that tasty nurse the old Yank had brought along with him? He could imagine either one of them out in the pagoda. Fresh, they were. Fresh and tasty. It would be easy enough to change and go out if he'd a mind for exploration. But whoever it was didn't linger; she went into the enormous glass building and there was lost from sight.

If the perennial breeze didn't allow for much heat, the same could not be said for the conservatory. Parakeets cawed amidst the branches of trees and vegetation from tropical climes. There were trays of lilies and stooping orchids bent over like shuffling men, their roots slippered in hanging clay vessels, damp moss between their feet.

Dr Quigg felt her brow bead up the minute the hothouse door shut. She removed her sun hat, which had come with her from the Transvaal, and used it to fan her face. She noted a series of dark iron pipes and put a testing hand upon each. Of course, that was it. Warm water—from a hot spring, perhaps? The boilers would have to be enormous otherwise. And then the path she had chosen to wander through this garden of Eden came to a sudden halt. A sturdy gate blocked her way, held fast by a solid bolt. 'No entry,' it told. 'Danger,' it cautioned on a second plate, and then, perhaps as an afterthought or sad untold experience, a third sign was screwed on below. 'Risk of fatality. Do not open. Don't say you haven't been warned!' Dr Quigg peered over the gate, but saw nothing to justify the signs. A second greenhouse stretched beyond, and beyond that she saw a third. It crossed her mind to slip the bolt, but whether from fear of censure or residual manners, or the nagging suspicion that three signs were more than a lot, she stayed her curious hand.

Drinks were served at six, as promised, though some of the guests had made an early start.

'Did you notice this when we came in?'

The great hall sported an enormous fireplace with a mantle fit to scale. The pelt of a tiger, head and teeth still attached, sprawled over a parquet floor. A hotchpotch of styles distinguished the chairs chosen seemingly for anything but comfort, no two alike. High on the walls hung portraits of the Blacks, ancestors looking down out of gilded frames. Taxidermied stag heads, their antlers dusty, gave the company a glossy eyed stare. There were Japanese vases, each as tall as a man, and an Oriental dragon in jade. There were

Zulu spears and a grand chiming clock that might have taken an elephant to move. All this menagerie was contained in one room, which was bounded by filigreed panelling, and none of it looked out of place.

Yet there was something else that did.

Andrew Sterling spilled a little of his glass as he gestured above the fireplace. 'I said, did anyone notice this when we all came in? Not what you might expect.'

Eleanor Grace was the closest. 'You know, Mr Sterling, I think you might be right. They do seem a little odd. Not quite in keeping with the rest of the decor, don't you think?'

There were ten of them when you counted, which everybody did. Ten green bottles. Common beer and soda bottles—it was hard to tell—their labels scrubbed or missing, and one or two of port or wine. No two were quite the same, but each was empty and clean, and they were spaced along the mantel ledge as one might display a collection.

'Perhaps Lord Black wants his deposits back?'

'Perhaps that's where he keeps the recycling?'

'Maybe they're given out as prizes with every deer that you bag.''

'Maybe they're the bathroom facilities!

'Maybe he uses them for target practice? Where is our host? We should ask him.'

Ten green bottles, hanging on the wall!
And if one green bottle should accidentally fall,
There'll be nine green bottles...

'Yes, yes, Dr Quigg. We're not all on a school trip here.'

'That ain't it!' DB contributed, recognizing the rhyme.

Ninety-nine bottles of beer on the wall,
Ninety-nine bottles of beer!
Take one down, pass it around,
Ninety-eight bottles of beer on the wall!

'Mr Bowers, please. Why does everything in America

have to be bigger?'

But since Lord Black had yet to appear, there was no one to shed light on this curiosity. Besides, at that moment, Mrs MacGregor, in her starched white apron of office, had just finished serving the last of the guests a drink, and as she did so a gong was sounded. All chat was interrupted. All heads turned.

'If I might have your attention, please.' It was Mr MacGregor, the gillie, who spoke. He had changed and was dressed as a butler. 'If I might have your attention,' he repeated. 'I have been instructed to read you a letter.'

'A letter?'

'What letter?' asked someone else.

'I have my directions from his Lordship, if it will please the party. The letter is in Lord Black's hand.' MacGregor lifted a manila envelope, closed and sealed in wax, on which *To my guests* was writ large.

No objections being raised—most in the great hall were startled, divided between amused, interested, and irritated—Mr MacGregor moved on and opened it.

My dear guests, it began. MacGregor's slow Highland drawl fell into the silence, his words reaching every cranny. The guests, whether seated or standing, craned forward to hear every sound.

My dear guests,

My apologies, foremost, for not being here to greet you, to speak to you in person on the purpose of my mind. You will understand soon enough.

Ten green bottles.

Henry Vail. I know you from my employ in Hong Kong. As corrupt a police officer of Her Majesty's colony as one could ill hope to meet. Your orders and actions cost the blood of innocents. Guilty as charged. Your sentence is death. The bailiff will take you away.

Andrew Sterling. Small man; little man; failure. Rather than apply yourself to grit and labour, you sought to extort monies from me. A healthy body must be free of parasites. I shall be cleansed of you.

Dr Frances Quigg. Entrusted with the care of the vulnerable, your treatments killed and maimed. Instead of repentance, you built a career. A work ethic is the only one you have. You and Mr Sterling should talk.

Mr Douglas Bowers III. Your media tentacles give golden tickets to the election fairground that is Congress. You incite warmongering and spread fear and distrust amongst the ignorant masses. You profit from your viewers through the graffiti that is advertising. My only regret is that the events to come will sell a great many of your newspapers. Even your death will see your aggrandizement. We can't have it all, it seems.

Eleanor Grace. Hollywood starlet. Black widow spider. Three husbands already you've helped to their graves and from each won a burgeoning wardrobe. It is not everyone that gets to know when their last performance will come. I hope the reviews of yours are kind.

Robert and Wendy MacGregor. Sad couple. You mourn the death of a child, yet it was you that put the handicapped boy down. Euthanasia is a game for the Gods. As is justice. And revenge.

Charles Fotheringham. Suspended license. Driving without due care and attention. Did you even know the name of that girl you ran down on that road? Newtonian physics, Mr Fotheringham; for every action, an equal and opposite reaction. Natural law will win out.

Sir Cyrus Gordon. Old friend. Did you bring the monkey or a caged polar bear? Are you decked out in satin and crepe? The women you bed, even the ones that you pay for, do you tell them of your HIV? Your late wife was surprised to hear. Fate gifts you an audience, a million followers, a modern-day apostle in the skin. Think about what you might have accomplished if there had been anything more to you! Waste defined the last century, old friend; the world will be a better place cleaned up. You enjoy a show, and so I gift you one. It promises to be your last.

Ten green bottles. All guilty as charged. Rats in a sinking ship. Dinner will now be served—Mrs MacGregor, please ask my guests to sit.

Chapter 4
Ten Green Bottles

IT WOULD BE NICE TO SAY THAT AN UNCOMFORTABLE SILENCE followed the reading of the letter, that Robert MacGregor's stilted narrative was met with reservation and dignity. Or perhaps not. Perhaps such an event should not be met with anything other than howling derision, with stunted fear, with incredulity, with anger. And so it was; whatever your soup flavour, the drawing room had it. Any composure had been spent on the reading, when all in the room listened quietly. True, there were murmurs, hushes, and groans, rumblings from deep in the throat. There were turned heads and furtive glances and distancing of the shoulders by fractions, but each in the room kept from interruption until the final word on the letter was out. Mr MacGregor read to the bottom, turned it over, saw nothing further, turned it back, looked it over again, and said by way of epigram. 'That's it. That's all there is. His signature. Nothing more.'

The scene, if you will, went as follows, but all of it happening at once. It was hard to tell who was in favour of what, or who bit their nails and felt small.

DB was quick out the blocks for a man of his age if not temper. 'God damn it!' He spoke to no-one and everyone. 'What the hell is the meaning of this?' No-one was forthcoming with an answer, but then no0one might have been listening, each digesting what they'd just heard. 'What the hell kind of lies is this lunatic spreading? He'll be talking to my lawyers real soon!'

'The gentleman doth protest too much, methinks,' Joan heard one of the other men say.

'The whole thing is in *very* bad taste' was a sentiment echoed by many.

'It's a game. It's just a big game. It's very rude to play with people this way.' It was young Mr Sterling who snivelled this point, talking to anyone he thought might be listening. But what struck Ms Hedringer more than the objectors was the others who were withdrawn or silent.

Dr Quigg, for one, clasping her sherry glass, had not seemed to move a muscle, while woolly young Mr Fotheringham, his hair in disarray, was staring at the ceiling for inspiration in the heavens of the frieze. Charlie's face was one of bemusement and surprise, his glasses slightly awry—when the extraordinary comes knocking on one's own door, some assume it's a mistake meant for the neighbours. Yet, Ms Hedringer keenly observed as she continued to look about the room that not everyone seemed so struck.

There was Mr Vail, the policeman—or so Lord Black's letter had said—the fellow appeared angered and hot; while Miss Eleanor Grace—three husbands, really?—was enjoying a smoke and a drink. The movie starlet, a few lines about her eyes, lifted her glass to salute. 'The Lord hates dull! Praise the Lord!' she toasted, unreciprocated, except perhaps for a grin from Cyrus. The man hadn't smiled since his monkey went swimming, but he managed a smile now.

'Did you notice,' Sir Cyrus said directly to Joan, catching her eye when she looked over his way, 'Did you notice that there were ten green bottles, but Black talked only of nine?'

Cyrus Gordon addressed the question to her but loud enough that many overheard.

'What? What's that?'

'Pass the letter, be a good sort, MacGregor.' Cyrus took the note from the gillie. He skimmed it. 'Vail, Sterling, Dr

Quigg, DB, Miss Grace, the MacGregors, Charlie, and myself. Nine.'

'Nine.'

'That's right, nine.' Cyrus folded the letter and tapped it in his hand. MacGregor waited, but he did not give it back.

'I don't see your name here, Ms Head Ringer.'

'Hedringer,' Joan corrected.

'Old Black left you off his list.'

'Well, that ain't any sort of a mystery.' DB had calmed somewhat. 'I brought her along unannounced.'

'You arrived at the boat after we went through this,' Dr Quigg explained. 'Mr Bowers requires a nurse.'

'Black didn't know she was coming?'

'She's my nurse, like the Doctor said…' But then DB halted what he was about to say, instead adding, 'Well, he might have had an idea she would be here.'

DB recalled that Black had asked for a girl, and hadn't he suggested Joan herself? Or was that something one of his editors had arranged? 'I ain't…that is, I ain't certain whether he knew or not.'

Joan felt nine sets of distrustful eyes weigh on her, but was saved by Mr MacGregor talking next.

'Pardon me for interrupting, sir, but might Lord Black not be the tenth bottle himself?'

'Why do you say that, man?'

'I only mean, sir, not meaning no disrespect, but I was given orders to lay a table for ten. You've all got your places, and Mrs MacGregor had the seating chart. Lord Black's got a place at its head. He was number ten; or number one, more like. There's no spot for Ms Hedringer at the table.'

'Black is dining here? You're expecting him to come?'

'I was told as much. He was in his room the past few days, but he likes his privacy and asked not to be disturbed.'

'Are you saying he's here, MacGregor? Lord Black is upstairs now?'

'I think so, sir. His door is locked from the inside, at any rate, and his light's been on these past two nights.'

As one, the party stirred.

'I think we should have a word with our host. Get to the bottom of this as soon as we can. Won't you lead the way to his room?' Cyrus turned towards the steps to the balcony.

'I'm sure he doesn't want any trouble, sir,' MacGregor defended.

'It's a little too late for that!'

⊂⊗⊗⊃

The room upstairs was locked.

'Is there another way in?' asked Cyrus, speaking for them all.

'That next door down, sir. That gives access to the bath chamber, and there's a door that goes inside from there too.' The hall bath door was tried but also found to be locked. They banged and called, but there was no answer.

'Fetch the key.'

'Are you sure?'

'Fetch the key, or I shall kick the thing down.'

Mrs MacGregor was summoned with her bunch of keys, and after knocking again, it was opened.

There were signs of habitation… but no Black.

'You didn't really expect him to be sitting here?'

'I'd say the fire was used less than a day ago.' Henry Vail bent up from the grate, wiping clean a sooty finger on his handkerchief. 'There's still a very faint heat from the coals.'

The bed looked like it had been slept in, and there was a pair of gentleman's patent dress shoes behind the door, while a dinner suit hung on the back of it, brushed and ready to be worn.

'Where is he, then?'

'Where else do you think, MacGregor?'

'I don't know, sir,' answered the gillie. 'I haven't seen all of the place myself.'

'What do you mean by that, exactly? What are you trying to say?'

'I haven't been here long enough to know it well yet, sir.'

'Don't know it? How long have you been here?'

'Just these three days.'

'Only three days!'

'Then where is the rest of the help?'

'There's just us, sir. All was readied. Nothing out of order. All smooth.'

'Look, it doesn't matter,' Cyrus interrupted. 'When was the last time you saw your employer?'

'I heard his Lordship up in here, sir. It's odd to think of, now you ask it, but truth is we never have seen him.'

'You never have?'

'We got the appointment by letter, and advance wages and all. Promise of a bonus, too. All instructions for preparations was clearly made out and available.'

'They were in an envelope in the kitchens.' Mrs MacGregor spoke up, behind them. 'It was all proper, sir. All arranged.'

'Look. Look over here!' It was Charlie Fotheringham who called the group's attention to a large writing desk. He'd been casting about and was sorry—but not really sorry—not to meet Lord Black in the flesh, and his eye had fallen on something.

'What have you got there?' DB asked, faster than the rest to crowd round.

'What do you think it means?' Charlie held it up.

'It could have been here a long, long time.' But no one sincerely thought so.

It was a drawing; a pen and ink cartoon. It filled half the sheet of a piece of paper torn from a spiral-bound book. It was a drawing of a dead rat, a dead rat stuck in a trap though the bait was not cheese but money. From the blotting paper and the gathered ink pots, it was clear that it had been created at that table. There was a caption to go along with it.

A is for Andrew, a paper-cut opener.

The lettering was plain; drawn rather than hand-written, or perhaps painted with a brush, and a bit blurry, as if it had leached.

A *is* for Andrew
a paper-cut opener.

Rats in a sinking ship, thought Charlie.

'That is not in very good taste,' said the doctor.

'Isn't one of us called Andrew?' asked Bowers.

'Mr Sterling! Where is Mr Sterling right now?'

They looked about them, around Black's room, but of Andrew Sterling there was nothing to be seen.

They hurried from the room on a shared sense of urgency, calling to the others below. Down the staircase to the drawing room they went, the tramp of anxious feet.

'A blackmailer and parasite, that's what Black's letter said.'

'I think he'd better be warned.'

'Has anyone seen Andrew?'

'Mr Sterling! Mr Sterling! Please come out! You need to know what we found.'

He was gone. No one could quite recall when they had

seen him last; the reading had been quite disruptive.

'He was sitting beside me when the letter was read. It gave him quite a shock.'

'That's his glass on the sideboard, I think. At least, I remember him drinking something like that. He's left it behind, wherever he's got to.'

'Mrs MacGregor, please show us to Mr Sterling's room immediately!' Cyrus had somehow taken charge. 'Everyone, please stay together!'

They followed Mrs MacGregor in a pack. Down the hall they went, staying on the ground floor, round the corner, two doors down, and there they stopped.

Knock, knock, knock. They didn't have to wait; the door swung in with the slightest push.

Sterling was there. Andrew Sterling, if that was his real name. He was kneeling on the floor, hunched over like a gatherer of sticks. It was obvious that there was nothing to be done; a knife was buried hilt-deep in his back. The blood from the wound covered half the floor, where it had puddled over the rug.

'Good God!' exclaimed DB.

'The poor man!'

Joan covered her mouth and looked away, wondering about how it would feel to have metal push in through your skin. She hadn't liked Mr Sterling—he'd always been looking at her.

Such a lot of blood there was. Where it had spilled onto the hardwood, it had sunk into the gaps of the parquet. Even now the blood still pooled and grew, leaking from the hole near the top of his back like a tap with a broken washer. They leaned closer, examining the wound, some from fear and morbid curiosity, others with a professional eye. If the jacket was rented, then the deposit was likely lost. It would need more than a couple of stitches to fix either it or its owner.

'I'd say it might indeed be a letter opener, judging by the handle.'

'Oh, don't touch it, please!'

But Cyrus did.

The kneeling body fell over.

Mrs MacGregor screamed. Her husband stood in shock and did not comfort her. It was Charlie Fotheringham who held her shoulders, who did the *there, there's* and soothing words.

Dr Quigg felt for a pulse at Sterling's neck, but shook her head shortly afterwards. Nothing we can do here.'

'Who would do such a terrible thing?' The answer was too obvious.

'Did anyone see anything after the letter was read?' asked Vail. 'Why did Sterling go to his room?' They all knew which letter he was talking about, but no one had an answer. His briefcase was on the carpet in front of him, open and visibly empty.

Dr Quigg had sense. She told the others to get out of the room and not to touch or disturb anything.

Most of the men bore serious faces, Sir Cyrus the only exception. 'The pen is mightier than the sword!' he crowed. He carried his laughter into the corridor.

'If you think that is funny, I do not,' said Dr Quigg crossly.

Cyrus didn't appear to give a fig. 'He got what he deserved!'

'You'd better explain what you mean by that.'

'His bag was chock full of blackmail letters—that's what I say happened. He brought them here to sell to Black. Obvious, isn't it? No? Black has done him in, and good for Black! Filthy sneak brought it all on himself.'

'And how could you know all this?' asked Charlie.

'Black's letter said as much! Good riddance is what I say.'

'Then you are the guest of a murderer, and you are witness to a crime,' Inspector Vail pointed out.

'Fellow was a weasel. Got exactly what he deserved.' Cyrus had brought his wine glass along, and he toasted the mouth-gaping corpse.

'That letter was full of lies!' DB spat.

'I'm not so sure it was,' Eleanor interjected. 'Of the things it mentioned and of which I am informed, all of them spoke true.'

'What do you say, Mr Sterling?' Cyrus called through the door. 'Do you regret what you did now?'

⟨⊗⊗⊗⊃

'Well, Vail? What about you? Are you a police officer or not?'

No one admitted to knowing Mr Vail or could vouch for him or his character; they only had Black's letter to go on, but he did not deny his profession.

'I have no jurisdiction. I retired a few years ago. I'm a guest here, same as you all are. It's pretty clear, though, what happened.'

'His briefcase is empty.' The dead man still held fast to the handle. 'Completely empty. Might have had nothing in it to start with.' They somehow all doubted that.

'Did any of you know him—Sterling here?'

Nobody claimed to. The first they'd ever seen the man was stepping onto the boat.

'His wallet's in his pocket. Where's his phone?'

'Don't touch anything.'

'I think the forensic team, whenever they arrive, will take a very dim view of any disturbance.'

'So we just leave him?'

'Unless you have a better idea?'

⟨⊗⊗⊗⊃

They gathered in the drawing room. Formality stood on its head. Charlie poured the housekeeper Mrs MacGregor a drink, as the woman looked paler than usual.

'Not for Mrs MacGregor,' her husband said.

'She can make up her own mind,' said Charlie.

'No, thank you.' Mrs MacGregor waved away the glass.

'Thank you, it's kind, but no.'

'Whatever you want.' He turned away. 'Here, get some of that down you.' Charlie offered Joan the single malt. 'You'll feel better. Calm you down.' Joan finished it all in a single gulp.

'I remember him, Sterling, carrying that briefcase along. He had it with him on the boat.'

There was consensus. He did have a briefcase in likeness to that one. 'And he carried it himself. Never left his side.'

'So we are to presume, given Black's accusations, that Andrew Sterling's career as a blackmailer was ill-chosen and short-lived? I suppose it explains Black's motive to do violence, by why would he involve all of us?'

'What do you mean, *involve*?'

'I mean that Black could have solved his Sterling problem quietly. Why do it here in front of us? Now we're all bound to give evidence, and everything will come out.'

'Maybe he needed a crowd,' suggested DB. 'Perhaps he needed a group of folks to lure his blackmailer here. Maybe Sterling was the suspicious sort.'

'But why the letter, telling us all? Why the drawing?' asked Dr Quigg.

'What drawing, if I may ask, sir?' Mr MacGregor hadn't seen it yet. DB had it folded up, and he now took the thing from out his pocket and passed it over the back of the couch. The rat caught in the trap. There was more than just a passing resemblance to what had happened in Sterling's room.

'Why bring Sterling here and kill him so publicly?' Dr Quigg asked again.

'A is for Andrew,' Charlie said.

'I think you've got the wrong end of the stick,' Vail replied. 'This isn't public, you shouldn't think that, no. This is a very, very private place. Black wants us here, we're a select audience, though why that might be I have no idea.'

'But we're all witnesses,' protested Quigg.

'Black doesn't care because he doesn't think any of us will be giving any evidence,' replied the Inspector.

'What do you mean?'

'Ten green bottles.'

'You don't think...?'

'He must be mad.'

'You think he means to kill us all?'

'Only you're the eleventh green bottle, Ms Hedringer. Unlucky you came along.'

'Hold on here!' DB rattled, as he pulled the cigar from his mouth. 'Jesus Christ, who did that!' He jabbed at the mantle with a fat ringed finger and at the mess on the floor underneath. Where there had been ten bottles—*ten* green bottles—one had been knocked over and had fallen.

'I didn't notice.'

'I never heard a thing.'

Yet one lay broken on the floor.

And if one green bottle
Should accidentally fall,
There'll be nine...

'Do you mind? We don't need to hear that.'

'Mrs MacGregor,' called Cyrus. 'Could you please have that mess swept up?'

'But the police!' objected Charlie.

'Damn the police. Where are they now?'

The trappings of civilization were all about them, yet at the same time felt far away. Mrs MacGregor made to fetch a pan and brush.

'Wait! Wait! Mr MacGregor, go with your wife, please,' Dr Quigg insisted. 'We're all green bottles here. Someone put a knife in that young man only minutes ago. No one goes anywhere alone.'

'Quite right, doctor,' approved the Inspector. 'Somebody is out there with a sick sense of humour, and we should be careful of what we all do.'

The MacGregors, man and wife, went out together.

'You really think so?' asked Eleanor. 'Do you really

think he means to hurt us?'

'Yes, I do,' said Vail.

'Then where the hell is Black right now?' asked DB. 'What kind of game is he playing? I'd be leaving right now if I had my helicopter. Best for all of us if we clear off quick.' He was trying to figure out if the island would be cheaper or more expensive with a convicted murderer putting through the sale. Something to ask his lawyers.

'I'm with you, Mr Bowers,' said Ms Hedringer through tight lips. 'I think I would like very much to go home.'

'Are you kidding?' interrupted Cyrus. 'This is a weekend you'll remember forever! Think of what you can tell your friends when you leak the grisly details."

'A man is dead; do I need to remind you?' Dr Quigg was not amused.

'I'll remember this trip all right, Mr Gordon.' DB rolled the unlit cigar to the other side of his mouth. 'I'm going to put it on the front pages when I get back. It'll be the lead on the six o'clock news.'

'It's what you make of it,' Cyrus persisted. 'Don't tell me you're not excited? It's life, folks! Beats the hell out of television. A lot less effort than reading the book.'

'They'll make it into a movie,' Eleanor spoke above the rest. 'I'm sure of the part. Only the men they cast will be better-looking...'

'And the women will be younger,' Vail cut her down.

'Jeesh. The policeman knows how to make friends,' said DB.

The MacGregors re-appeared and swept.

'Put it in a paper bag. Who knows? Maybe there are fingerprints. Don't touch anything by hand.'

'What about the rest of them?'

'Throw them out!' DB spoke up. 'Break 'em first. Smash 'em and bury 'em. I've had enough of that crap.'

'You can't,' Quigg said again, exasperated. 'Haven't you heard of such a thing as *evidence*?'

'Then stick them in a box. Put them out.'

It should have been easy; it might even have been a good idea; but a pagan sense of mysticism had somehow entered and settled on the room. They did not see it arrive. If it snuck in under the door or seeped in from the window frame, they were none the wiser. It was not tactile, it had no smell or taste, yet the association carried a mass—there was a weight within the room. Something tied the bottles on the mantelpiece to their own individual fates. Nine fragile green glass bottles, each perched atop the fireplace ledge.

'Maybe just leave them there for now.'

The MacGregors were sent to rally food. No one objected to that.

◁∞∞▷

'We should get out of here as soon as we can. Contact the real police.'

'There must be another boat we can take. Even something with oars.'

But no one could remember seeing a boat, either moored in the bay or pulled up on the shore.

'There must be one somewhere. There must.'

'When is the *Selkie* coming back?' Dr Quigg inquired of their ride over. Had it really only been that morning?

'Not due back before the end of the week, weather permitting. That's what the skipper said,' Charlie answered.

'Surely we can call? There's got to be a number.'

There was a universal delving into pockets and a collection of mobile phones came out. DB didn't carry one; nor, it appeared, did the MacGregors. But there was no service for anyone.

'Well, that's a lot of use.'

'Is there a satellite phone?' Charlie suspected the answer before he asked.

Inspector Vail picked up an old wired phone similar to the one in his room. He pressed the receiver up and down and got a series of clicks. No one was picking up.

'Internal, I believe,' Cyrus told him.

'We could try building a signal fire,' Joan suggested.

'We are hardly marooned, dear girl! What's all the panic about? A roustabout gets his check cashed in; why let it ruin the weekend?' Cyrus passed a whisky sour to a grateful Eleanor Grace, and she took it with an immodest smile.

'They burn the heather here, miss. Clears the fields,' MacGregor the gillie informed her. The staff were clearing plates.

'What are you saying, Mr MacGregor? Why does any of that matter?'

'Good for encouraging new growth each year. The cover keeps the grouse coming back.'

'He means that smoke won't mean a damn thing to anyone. It's the most natural thing in the world.'

'I think, perhaps, we're all getting a little jumpy,' Charlie suggested. 'Cyrus might be right. Black obviously had it in for Mr Sterling, but that might be the end of it all.'

'You're not serious?'

'End of everything, all right.'

'It's getting on for nine o'clock. It's bound to be dark soon. Without a phone, we're not getting off before morning. We should take precautions tonight.'

'You don't have to tell me that.'

'What about the guns?'

'Guns?'

'What do you mean?'

'I mean what I said. What about them? This is a lodge—there's bound to be a gun room. Black is out there. Don't you think it's wise to arm ourselves?'

They went as a scrum.

'Really, Mr MacGregor, you should have said something earlier.'

'I didn't think about it much, sir.'

But when they got there, it was to find disappointment. Bandoliers and gun bags were hung in the dry room beside myriad boots and coats, but the guns themselves, if there were any, were locked in an enormous safe.

'It's like the bloody *Bismarck*.'

'Mr MacGregor, sir. The key?'

'I don't have any key, sir.'

'You don't have the key?'

'I was presuming Lord Black had the key. Nothing out of order there. I brought my own gun along.'

'You mean *you've* got a gun?'

'I'm the gillie, sir. I should hope so. Not much of a gamekeeper without one.'

'And did you lock it up?'

'As I said, sir. I didn't have the key.'

'Good lord.'

'But what about the gun safe?'

It wasn't to be moved and it wasn't to be breached, so they decided to foul the lock. They filled the lock with fishing line weights and melted them with a small propane torch; it was the best they could manage.

'That was an expensive safe,' MacGregor pointed out.

'If we're not getting in, then no one is.'

'Unless his Lordship emptied it first.'

'We don't really know each other very well, but if we look out for each other, we should be fine. Lock your doors, that sort of thing. Tomorrow in the daytime, I suggest we have a really good search. There's nine of us here, counting Ms Hedringer and the staff. We'll beat the bushes and flush Black out. He can't hide from all of us. We'll keep an eye out for any passing boats, too. If we keep our heads, this will all work out, and then the police can take care of Sterling.'

It sounded like the sort of plan that might assuage the doubts of the many, regardless of the facts. Charlie Fotheringham, hearing no nay-sayers, lifted his glass to seal the deal. 'We're agreed, then?'

No one said no.

And really, what else *could* they do?

But Charlie was wrong on a few things. It being July and so far north on this remote island of the British archipelago, it scarcely got dark at all. True, the sun dipped below Beinn Sted in the west, the island's shattered mountain bit off by the Atlantic that blocked the worst of its storms, but the sky never seemed to give up on a sunset, and only faded to a faerie twilight—a world in shadow and grey. Unfamiliar noises and disquiet of the soul kept more than one guest awake.

Chapter 5
The Island

DAWN CAME EARLY FOR THOSE USED TO MORE SOUTHERN climes, yet such was the opacity of the double hung curtains that this was missed by more than one sleepy head. There were others who were grateful for the miserable light and the silhouette of the distant mainland across the churlish sea. Dangers faced alone in the wee dark hours are twice the weight and worry; they are halved by mornings and company.

⊂⊗⊗⊃

Breakfast solved the predicament of hunger, but advanced little sustenance towards hope.

'You slept all right, Ms Hedringer?' Charlie Fotheringham was laying into a plate that might have been bacon and eggs, and he stood aside to offer her a place.

'Scarcely a wink, Mr Fotheringham.' She accepted tea in a china cup with just a spot of milk. 'The house rattles. It is incumbent with noise. I heard Lord Black at my door last night with every groan of wind.'

'You poor thing!'

'You will think me weak. The bathroom was just down the hallway, but I was too scared to turn my door key.'

'Oh, Ms Hedringer, you should have said. I have an enormous room with a bathroom en suite. You shall have that room tonight. I insist.'

'Thank you, Mr Fotheringham, you are very kind, but I plan on being halfway to London before the end of today.' Joan Hedringer had an oatcake to go along with her tea. Her hopes for travel, as things turned out, would be disappointed in the extreme.

⬤⬤⬤⬤⬤

Eleanor Grace had barely taken a bite out of her toast.

'Do you mind if I join you?' Charles Fotheringham was taking the seat as he asked. Mrs MacGregor, walking by, was asked to bring the coffee pot—'Coffee for you too, Miss Grace?'—but she declined. Charles crossed his legs, brushing his trousers free of imaginary crumbs, and fidgeted with the juggling a spiral notepad in one hand and a fountain pen in the other. He put both down on the table and hauled out a half-empty beaten sleeve of French cigarettes that he'd bought over a year ago. The label said they were unfiltered. He offered one. Eleanor declined but took one of her own, which cost four times as much.

'I didn't see you smoke yesterday, Mr Fotheringham,' Eleanor observed.

'Yesterday I wasn't a smoker.'

'Well, welcome back to the dark side. Something has to kill you.'

'Not the week we had all planned.' It was Charles' way. His technique. Really a stalling tactic. He would circumnavigate his real purpose, more comfortable with himself and what he might ask next by establishing a veneer of 'shared souls'.

'No, Mr Fotheringham. Not the week we had planned at all.'

'Please call me Charlie.'

'Okay, Charlie, I'm happy with that. So what do you

think is going on?'

Charlie was not ordinarily susceptible to the fear of an attractive woman, but he was getting twinges of it now. Eleanor, ten years his senior at least—her age was never admitted, even in her obituary—carried the confidence of her natural good looks and hid her own growing private reservations. She was well turned out and allowed her native English accent a liberty outside of the studio.

'I wouldn't be concerned,' he confided, 'if we were all on the mainland and could drive off. Pull out a mobile and call the cops. Phone for a taxi or two. I admit there is something about being cooped up here that lends one an empathy towards chickens.'

'You think the woods are full of foxes? Are you feeling vulnerable? Is that it, Charlie?' She wore a smile on half her face as if nothing else was new.

'At least one fox. And I don't quite get his game.'

'This would be your employer we're talking about?'

He held his lighter for her. He wondered where she had heard that from, but wasn't surprised it had come out.

'Lord Black, yes. I'm supposed to be writing his biography.'

'Black is paying you to write his own book?' Charles thought he detected an amused tone from Miss Grace. 'And who is he paying to read it?'

The coffee pot arrived to save him. It came with a small jug of milk—no cream—and Demerara sugar loose in a blue china bowl with a doll's house spoon to serve it. When the rituals of serving were complete, Charlie had another go.

'Miss Grace'—he was hoping for the Eleanor, but so far it had not been offered—'Might I ask how it is you got to know Lord Black? He's hardly one to attend gala events or movie openings. What brought you out to the island this week, if you don't mind me asking the question?'

She took her time before answering, drawing once, then twice on her cigarette, her untouched toast colder. Charlie cautioned himself against stolen glances, though he had noted her cream stockinged ankles. It was bad enough when she picked out loose tobacco with fingernails the colour of dark cherry, and her tongue cleaned her bottom lip after. The lady was a distraction.

'Do you mean to tell me, Mr Fotheringham, that you are still going ahead with this book?'

He had already given thought to that very question. It had kept him awake half the night, in fact, but rationalizing it, as he did now with Miss Grace, he didn't think he had anything to lose.

'You asked me who is going to read it. If I am writing the biography of a madman and killer, then the answer is everyone.'

Miss Grace seemed to warm to him. 'Yes, Charlie. I think you've got something there. The public has only one condition—celebrity can never be boring.'

'Then you'll be in my book, Eleanor?'

'Lord Black's book, Mr Fotheringham.'

'As you say, Miss Grace.'

CXXXD

Dr Quigg was served by Mrs MacGregor, who dished from silver platters. Breakfast was in the morning room, tea and coffee to one side. There was no fruit or yoghurt, to Frances' dismay. She jabbed her fork at cooked tomatoes.

That slut, Miss Grace, was talking to Fotheringham, and had the impertinence to smoke in the house. Mr Bowers was at an adjacent table, a dirty plate in front of him as yet uncleared of seconds. The man was reading a two-day old newspaper, an unlit cigar balanced between his teeth. She imagined the stench from his mouth. Mr Bowers shook the paper violently every time he turned its pages.

'Do you own that one too?' the doctor asked him, sitting down in the seat across.

'Not yet.' He smiled at her amicably, and then the paper came up like a screen.

Dr Quigg wasn't sure if he was being funny. The ignorant man read on, and she looked around. What was that reserved policeman doing, sitting with his back to the wall? He was watching them, watching all the others in the room—the man was violence dressed in a shirt. The thought had only come to Dr Quigg when the dark, pouchy eyes found hers. He was looking at her sitting with Mr Bowers. Frances dropped her gaze.

'Tea, ma'am?' asked the mousy Mrs MacGregor. She turned the cup up on the saucer and poured at the doctor's affirmative.

Mr Gordon was the last to show up. Everyone was now there from last night.

'All right. If I can have your attention?' It was Charlie Fotheringham standing up, Sir Cyrus's arrival his cue. He had finished saying whatever it was that had made Miss Grace laugh out loud. 'All right, look everybody, we've had a night to think on it, and as I see it, not much has changed. Lord Black has still not appeared, and Mr Sterling, poor fellow, is still dead. That letter Mr MacGregor read has made threats to all of us.

DB folded his paper and pushed his plate away. Inspector Vail crossed his legs and put his hands behind his head. Sir Cyrus Gordon turned in his seat to give his full attention to Mr Fotheringham.

'It's time we did something about it,' Charlie continued. 'I propose we stick to the plan of last night—we find Black before he finds us.'

'How about we just go home?' asked Dr Quigg, to the point.

'That too!' he answered, annoyingly agreeable. But without a boat worthy to risk the sea, I believe we're safer here until help comes to us. We are fed and sheltered in this house until Friday at the latest.'

'Friday!' DB objected. 'You're asking us to sit around until then?'

'I'm not saying that...'

'But Black is out there! That's a week away. We're help-less sitting here.' Ms Hedringer was all nerves.

'Please don't get upset,' Charlie asked the room.

Dr Quigg gave the young woman a look of scorn. *Pull yourself together, girl.* If there was one thing she couldn't stand, it was emotions clouding decisions.

'It's very possible there's a boat somewhere, even a row-ing boat or something. And someone else, a farmer perhaps, might live somewhere else on the island. These things we don't know about yet, and that's the point—we hardly know anything at all. We need to find out, that's what I'm suggest-ing. We need to find anything or anyone who can assist us and help get all of us to safety.' Charlie nodded his head to encourage the others. 'I think we need to take this opportu-nity to look around and establish the facts.'

'What are you saying, Mr Fotheringham? You want us to go out and explore?'

'Exactly,' answered Charlie. 'That's just what I want. We need a thorough search of the place, both this island and the house. If Black's a lunatic, as some of us suppose, then he's hiding around here somewhere. We should team up and run him to ground. Get the better of him.'

'How do you think we'll do that?'

'I propose we split into threes. Three groups of three, I mean, and find out all we can. That way we can cover more ground, and still look out for each other. None of us came to harm last night when we had our eyes open for each oth-er. Black caught us unawares with Sterling, and I don't see that happening again. Unless anyone has a better idea, that's what I think we should do.'

There were no objections.

⊙⊠⊠⊠⊙

Inspector Vail couldn't quite figure out how he'd ended up with this pair of crazies. Mr and Mrs MacGregor were with him, each as annoying as the other. For the life of him, Vail couldn't figure out why Mrs MacGregor kept going on about eggs.

'They'd be nice for a breakfast tomorrow, so they would.'

The Inspector couldn't help himself. 'What on earth are you rambling on about?'

It was meant to be that pretty Joan girl, and Mr MacGregor to fill out their three, but the plans had been changed when a disagreement broke out and the American had insisted on his nurse.

It didn't make sense. It wasn't good planning. The MacGregors, however new they were, still remained the best intelligence they had. The couple had more time on the island than the rest of them combined. Yes, the fellow with the drowned monkey had said he'd been to the house before, but Henry didn't imagine him straying too far from the decanter, and no one knew a place like the workers. It was in the cellars, workshops, and boat sheds that their salvation would be found. The MacGregors should have been split up, the pair of them. This search was going all wrong.

'Mr Bowers and Mr Fotheringham will take Ms Hedringer up island. Mr Vail and the MacGregors are responsible for the local shore. The rest of us will turn over this house, every book and paper and crumb!'

Cyrus was very pleased with himself. Getting the adorable Miss Grace on his team was exactly what he had wanted. Let the old maid, Dr Quigg, tag along. No wet feet or trudging miles for him if they had to stay indoors. The teams gave assurances—they would reconnoitre in the drawing room by no later than four. Six hours to explore with Eleanor! What a lovely treasure hunt.

The third of the expedition that was Mr Charles Fotheringham, biographer emeritus; Mr Douglas Bowers III, dined with five presidents; and Joan Hedringer, uninvited guest, had an interesting start to their day. Almost immediately they discovered an automobile. 'It can't be running?'—and yet, beyond the odds, it proved to. True, it wasn't the only transportation on the island—the MacGregors had the keys to a serviceable tractor that might outrun the lame—but this was entirely another thing. She was a short, sporty girl, an aberration to the terrain, a two-seater Austin-Healey with a narrow bench in place of rear seats. The years, it seemed, had been kind to her, under a tarp in an unused stable. The near absence of tracks, let alone roads on the island, only made its attendance more spectacular.

The car, whose discovery catalyzed excitement, was, regrettably, still only a car. It was not, as it were, a boat. But might it not help find a boat? That train of thought, soon after expressed, led to the first of the morning's arguments.

The expedition was charged with two purposes; the first, to ascertain the number and viability of all routes of egress—how to get off the island; the second, to flush out Lord Black, their complicated host, and capture the devil if they could.

The car proved a sticking point. Judging from the dust and one soft tire, it hadn't been driven in some time. The idea that Black had used the thing recently was quickly stricken off. But should they use it themselves?

Charlie Fotheringham was not a fan. 'There's no way we'll get the jump on Black if we're blaring around in that thing.' It was an obvious point. There was no reason to suppose Black was deaf; he'd hear them from a mile off. 'Leave the thing where it is.'

DB was in favour of using it. 'Forget Black, I tell you,' he countered. 'If our host wants to stay hidden from us, there ain't no way we're going to smoke him out. You think without out dogs we'll flush him out, set up like he is on his own island?' Neither Charles nor Joan knew much about dogs, other than you picked up after them. 'In the car, we'll be able to cover a lot more of this rock and see if there's another way off.'

DB was no Davy Crockett; his outdoorsman years were long gone. Why they had agreed to let the old man and his cane explore the island with them nagged at the back of Charlie's mind. The old fellow would have been better tasked to the house, with its flat floors and banister rails. Charlie looked sideways at DB, his opinion growing worse by the minute. DB was portly, unfit, short of breath, given to tobacco—and his handmade shoes, from what Charlie could tell, were not close to being broken in.

'It's a fool that walks when the carriage is free,' DB pronounced with confidence.

'We can cover more ground with the car, Charlie. It does seem a terrible waste.' Joan stepped in, and spoke aside to Charlie when DB wasn't listening. 'Can you see him clambering over these hills? He's not as young as you might think.'

'He's an anchor. We should leave him behind.'

'No, Charlie. We stick together. We'll all be much safer like this.'

'Will we? Will we be safer if we don't find Black?' But Charlie knew he had lost round one.

Every book and paper and crumb was what Cyrus had said. Apparently every detailed search required a prolonged start at the drinks cabinet. Mr Gordon was on his knees and industrious, raising the occasional find to inspect its label in better light, putting it aside to spelunk further.

'Champagne?' he offered.

'It isn't chilled.'

'Be a dear and fetch a glass.'

'I hardly think this is appropriate, Mr Gordon. We have been tasked with a duty, and it would be irresponsible not to complete it sober.' Dr Quigg was pinch-lipped after that.

'Party pooper!' The cork popped and gave off an echo. The house rang hollow with so few of them in it; only the march of a pendulum was distinct. Cyrus filled a glass and passed it to Eleanor after Dr Quigg refused, and then filled another for himself.

'Here's to life,' he toasted.

'Sure beats the alternative,' Eleanor replied. They drank. Miss Grace threw her head back, finishing her glass, and Sir Cyrus watched her neck as she swallowed. Eleanor wiped the inside of her glass and licked it off her finger.

'You are a treat,' Cyrus complimented.

'Why don't we bring the bottle?'

Dr Quigg was not as disapproving as she let on—let the fools have their party. She considered herself smarter than either of them, and in that she was probably right. No one was going to take her unawares, she thought, and when they got moving it was the doctor who led, her ears peeled for the slightest sound.

⊂⊗⊗⊃

'How many more of these are down here?' Inspector Vail asked the MacGregor man. They were going through a couple of disused outbuildings they had passed on their way from the quay. No Black, no boat, so far. The tension and excitement that had marked the morning search had petered out when the rain came on. The sheen of tiny drops was only a mist, but it put a gloss on everything. A smir, Mrs MacGregor called it. You didn't even know you were getting wet. The cold stole up on you, unbidden.

The clutter of little houses were in a terrible state; slate roofs in disrepair, stone and mortar walls fallen in. Two of the buildings had window sills easily three feet thick, while the others hadn't so much as a door, and you had to pick your way in through the walls. Weeds grew up through floors once cared for. Clearly there were no families to sweep them now.

'They were not no likely crofts,' MacGregor told him, who recognized their sort.

Crofters—tenant farmers who eked out a living between shore fishing and hard farms. Seaweed harvested from the beach would fertilise small fields. The families that lived there had coaxed subsistence crops; turnip, potato, barley. And where were they now? They had been chased out two hundred years ago, sent away to scrape a living somewhere else. Families pawned what they had for a third-class ticket and took plank onto emigré ships, and those that stayed were led by need and drawn into the cities. Industrial Britain had called to them, and Britain's poor had answered—good news for the Black family either way.

'If I were to guess, sir,' Mr MacGregor surmised, 'the castle workers that raised Taigh Dubh might have lived here after that.' Whether MacGregor had a nose for history or was just making conversation, he was right enough again. The house when it was built had been a work in progress for half a dozen years. Masons had laid it stone by stone, each block cut by hand. They had lived here with their wives and children, scores of tradesmen and labourers.

'I don't want a bleeding history lesson, MacGregor. I just asked you how many there were.' Inspector Vail had his revolver underneath his overcoat in case anyone jumped out at him. The gillie, too, carried a gun—his shotgun, breach broken, resting under one arm, the most natural thing in the world.

'Doesn't look like no one's been here in a while,' the gillie said in his soft lilting tongue that was getting on Inspector Vail's nerves. MacGregor's tendency to double negatives was grating on him too. *You'll not be needing your tea, no, sir?* Vail was careful to let him go first.

Vail didn't bother to answer. He knew—had long suspected—that a search of the property this far away was an utter waste of their time. What were they thinking? *Whoever had offed that grubber Sterling wasn't camping out in the wild.*

Did they think that Black had herded them together like this only to hide out in a cave? No, no. Henry Vail was under no such illusions. Lord Black had brought them to the island with something specific in mind. Black had wanted them to hear the pantomime of the letter, see the green bottles, bear witness to Sterling's farcical death—a letter opener for a blackmailer! Black had wanted to see their faces, Vail was certain of it, and smell the whiff of their fear. Had he been there last night? Undoubtedly. He had looked down on them, perhaps, from the shadows of the balcony behind the balustrade railings upstairs or from behind a crack in the billiard room door, watching as they called for Andrew. Maybe he was the shape behind a suit of armour in the hall, listening as their voices cried out through the corridor. Black was everywhere, watching them. Perhaps he was watching them now. Henry laughed without explanation. Mr and Mrs MacGregor stopped what they were doing and gave the policeman a look.

Black must have been there, Vail rationalized; otherwise how would he have known when the coast was clear to sneak in with the knife? With the letter read, everyone running upstairs, who would have noticed who remained below? There was certainly limited opportunity; they'd been gone five minutes at most. Had Black been waiting in Sterling's room, *or*—Henry pulled up; this new idea scared him more—or had Black actually been there all along, and the murderer was one of them?

Inspector Vail stopped walking. *What did Black even look like?* He had never actually met the man.

Henry Vail. I know you from my employ in Hong Kong. As corrupt a police officer of Her Majesty's colony as one could ill hope to meet. Your orders and actions cost the blood of innocents. Guilty as charged. Your sentence is death. The bailiff will take you away.

The letter was not wrong—he had worked for the Blacks through the Hong Kong handover and for the Guangzhou Free Zone concessions. He had handled a few contract irregularities and passed some intelligence down the line. An Inspector of Police, he had helped a few union agitators into the hands of the mainland authorities. Nothing that he was ashamed of. Nothing that anyone else wouldn't do. But had he ever come face to face with Black? No. Never, in all of those years. What was more, he had never even seen a photograph of the man who had sent the red envelopes his way. It was a family company, not beholden to public shareholders. Lord Black was a bit of a recluse. What mattered was that his money was good.

'Inspector Vail, sir...' Mr MacGregor brought him back to the moment.

'Yes, Mr MacGregor?' Vail turned.

'Nobody's living down here, sir. Is there somewhere else you'd like to look next?'

'No. I agree, this is a waste of time, though it has been valuable in other ways.'

'Sir? I'm sorry. I don't quite catch your meaning.'

'Meaning there's a danger in assuming too much, MacGregor. We should not presume to assume.'

'If you says so, sir. If you do.' MacGregor held his own opinion of the Englishman, but he didn't air it here.

They stayed a moment in the relative shelter before stepping out again. A third of the wall was broken and missing, and they looked through it down to the shore. Vail could see the waves from the channel fetch higher, and though MacGregor knew it was the wind and not the tide, proximal companionship had not succeeded in weathering their distrust, and so each kept their mind to themselves.

⬡⬡⬡

Taigh Dubh was two storeys plus her lofts, built around an open courtyard of perennial gardens and a carp pond. Aside from the great hall where they had come in, the drawing room with its green bottle collection, the dining room where they had breakfasted, the billiard room which a few of the men had grown fond of, and the oak balustraded balconies, most of the rest of house was chamber rooms of varied greatness and sizes. There were the kitchens, of course, with larders and a cold room; a boiler with its coal cellar that required shovelling if the heating was on; and there was a provision for the generation of electricity that appealed to modern green times.

'The blighter actually built a dam that makes the lights go on!' Cyrus thought he was doing them a favour by trying to convey the marvel of electrical illumination, the magic of it all, to his eye. 'He's got a lake or loch, somewhere inland, likely up amongst the hills. A couple of turbines and a few miles of copper wire and all the comforts of modern times!' Dr Quigg, a woman of science, could have drawn him a blueprint for the dynamo. Miss Grace, despite what she might choose to play, was no one's fool either. She had land in California that her second husband had left her, and she kept a close eye on the price of water licenses. Her orchards were irrigated from the Colorado by way of the Hoover Dam.

'Fascinating, Cyrus. Fascinating. But why won't my hairdryer work?'

'It's over a hundred years old, my dear Eleanor. It was built in the early 1900's. The power isn't standard for today, but think how before its time it was! Free electricity for over a century!'

'You do enthuse, Cyrus, you do.'

Everything about Eleanor annoyed her, Dr Quigg reflected. The way she flattered the man. 'Don't worry, dear. Your hairdryer is a bust, but the mirrors still work, so you can keep yourself amused.'

'Cyrus, what is the old girl saying now?'

They had worked their way around to the second floor. The anticipation in each turning handle kept them from falling out entirely.

'This one is my room,' Eleanor told them. 'There was no one but me here this morning.'

'Might we have a look? Check under the bed? Better safe than sorry, don't you think?'

'Is that how you get into all the girls' rooms? I thought you could do better than that.'

But Eleanor did not refuse, and she unlocked it with her key. The room was spacious and light, done in yellow and ivory, south-facing and on a corner to the bay. Light rain fell on the windows outside, yet from somewhere the sun still shone through.

'Twice the size of mine,' Dr Quigg noted. She observed a dressing table heaped high with clothes.

There was a whiff of the continent about the place, something anti-Presbyterian. Empire French striped wallpaper, fireplace mouldings bearing fleur-de-lis, the curve to table legs. It was a princess grotto with frilly bedding. Of course there was a four-poster bed.

'Have you seen the clock?' Eleanor waved them over. 'It only has one hand—just the hour hand,' she told them, amused. 'There was no minute hand for the late Lady Black; the world conformed to her sense of time.'

'You like that idea, don't you?'

'Of course.'

Cyrus was impressed. In his best American impersonation, 'I've got to get me one of those.' It wasn't clear if he meant the clock or Miss Grace.

But of the present Lord Black, there was no sign.

Charlie dropped the clutch and slipped into second, spinning the wheels as he took the next corner. A series of switchbacks up to the ridge was proving a lot of fun. Joan shrieked from the back bench as DB hooted, the thrill of the drive grown contagious. 'Mr Toad rides again!'

'What's that you're saying there, Moley?'

Charlie had to admit he was glad for the ride. The valley rose and the single track went with it, climbing towards

the heart of the island. They were at the feet of Beinn Sted —
the anvil mountain — chewing the miles up the glen.

'What's that?' Charlie called. He hit the brakes, stopping
them over a gully. Below them they could make out a chimney and a steep roof that covered a low-walled shack. It was
a small house — they could only see it now, as it had been
hidden from view from below.

'Anyone home, do you think?'

'He'd have heard us already.'

'Be ready then, we should check it out.' He turned the
car off and pocketed the key.

It was simple refuge and unoccupied, provided with water
from a nearby stream and serviced by an outside toilet. It
proved a disappointment. Worse, it turned their guts.

'Do you smell that?'

'What is it?'

'Something nasty.' Charlie pulled his jacket collar up
over his nose. He pressed his thumb to the latch that held
the door, pushed it and went in.

A bench and table carried a camping stove while a candle, ribbed with hard dribbled wax, had been propped in
a bottle for light. There was dust in a couple of glasses and
a couple more that were clean. And the hanging smell of
death.

Rack upon rack of rotting birds hung like a headdress
from the ceiling, a hook through each of their beaks. Some
were fly-chewed down to the bone, mere bags of skin and
feathers. Their eyes were maggot-eaten and their tongues
chewed out, looking so much like deflated balloons. Those
were the okay ones, merely upsetting, for they had bloated
and burst long ago. The others, fresher, disturbed by the vis-
itors, came to life amid a cloud of flies.

'Leave the door open.' Charlie batted the air, trying to
clear the pests.

The deer were different altogether.

'Jesus Christ!' DB covered his mouth, Joan retreated for

fresh air, and Charlie took a hesitant step into the bloody larder.

The stag was crucified. Thick railway nails had been hammered through its forelegs, pinning the creature to the beam. Someone had split it open from its neck to its anus and let gravity do the rest. Its pluck hung out—heart, liver and lungs—a gory stew had dripped onto the floor. Entrails flopped like a dropped bag of wool and had taken insect hosts. The flagstone floor beneath the deer was a sauce of mould and fluid. The animal's head lay rag-doll back, its antlers still in its skull.

'Look at this.' Charlie pointed, hand held across his nose to ward the stench. Bloody footprints led to the door; human feet had walked through the mess and out to the island beyond.

Chapter 6
Broken Glass

'MacGregor.'

'Yes, sir?'

'The letter said you had a son. It mentioned he was disabled.' Inspector Vail broke the subject straight out.

There was a pause.

'Handicapped, sir. Yes, sir, it did. The letter said such a thing.'

'It said the pair of you did him in.'

MacGregor locked the stock to the shotgun barrel but kept it pointed at the ground. Mrs MacGregor, who followed like a mule, broke into snottery sobs.

Her dog-duty husband riled. 'That'd be none of your business, Mr Vail. I don't much care if you're a policeman or not.' MacGregor was red-faced but his voice was steady. 'It's lies, all lies, and the subject is closed. No good to talk of such things.'

Vail thought the man kept it pretty much under control; but they all knew he had been given his answer.

⸎⸎⸎

The cart track kept going further up the glen, and they followed it slowly in the car. There was no escaping the change of mood that had settled on them since the game hut. The slopes of Beinn Sted now presented a menace where before there had been none. Whoever had last been in that hut might have taken this very road.

'Are you all right?' Charlie asked. Joan looked pale. 'I would have thought a nurse had seen worse.'

'No one should get used to that. That poor animal back there.'

'You eat hot dogs, Mr Fotheringham?' asked DB. 'I don't picture you for a vegetarian. You eat hot dogs at the ball game?' Charlie gave DB a look, not sure if he was making fun.

'Why did they get left like that, Charlie? Who would do such a thing?' Joan was visibly shaken.

'A question for our gamekeeper, MacGregor—unless he's new, like he said. I don't know what's going on, Joan. Nothing in there was fresh.'

'What a god-damned country,' said DB. 'No wonder the Romans stayed away.'

'Maybe it's only a case of neglect,' Charlie suggested. 'Hunting's very common in these parts.'

'I don't think what we saw could be described as *normal*.'

'Who would do something like that?'

'Someone was there,' Charlie pointed out.

'Yes, but where are they now?' asked Joan.

None of them had an answer to that. They continued on the road, eyes alert.

⬤⬤⬤⬤

'Why do you think he's doing this, Cyrus?' Eleanor asked.

'Having a little fun.'

'I don't see the amusement in any of this,' remarked Dr Quigg acidly.

'That's because you're a dried-up prune who has forgotten what life is for,' said Eleanor who'd hours ago had enough of the woman. 'You live solely for what's between your ears and ignore what's between your thighs.'

'I should hope so! Floozy.'

'Call me a floozy again and I'll slap you hard. You hear? I don't care how old you are. You'll get it, you old witch. Don't think you won't.'

'Oh, girls, please. Give it all a rest,' Cyrus yawned, and offered the ladies a cigarette.

'I haven't smoked in forty years.' Dr Quigg turned him down with pride.

'Is there a problem that you don't have?'

Cyrus held a match for Eleanor, who detained his arm with her hand.

Cyrus spoke. 'I understand you're uptight, Frances— might I call you Frances? No? More's the pity, but there it is. This can't be your sort of thing, I imagine, a weekend with people of spirit. Out of your comfort zone, I understand that, and then a blighter goes off and gets killed!' He laughed.

'I would hardly have thought the recent events were a matter to inspire amusement.'

'Exactly, Doctor! Because you are *that* sort of person. But there you would be wrong. It is as old Black said himself— the very best thing that could happen to a party. It is very funny, in a certain light.'

'Young Mr Sterling might take umbrage.'

'Young Mr Sterling was a toad. They poison toads in Australia; it's overrun with the things. In Argyll, apparently, they are stabbed.'

'Why do you presume to know Black's mind? How can we know why he did this or that? Why would you think it's fun?'

'He's having his sport with us, Frances. You have to believe it's so. This is an island for hunting. Deer and fish and now us. It sounded clear enough in his letter, but the fellow is obviously unhinged. Take care, Dr Quigg, take care!' Cyrus pointed his cigarette at the woman, the smoke laying a track through the air. 'Whatever's going on here, Black has schemed it. There's some planning behind our week here.'

'And you don't fear him for that?'

'I'm a modern man. I am open to experience. It is as Black's letter said—I am thrilled. Gets the blood pumping. Makes one feel alive. Anything but boring, please. You can't say he's giving you *that*.'

Doctor Quigg was taking it in, clearly not happy with the mood.

'Eleanor, what do you think?' Cyrus asked.

'Honey, I'm fit to be tied, but you'll protect me, I'm sure. So long as there's something to drink.'

'This is a waste of time up here,' said Cyrus. 'I'll tell you that for sure.'

'Then let's please go back downstairs and wait.'

'Certainly not,' said Quigg. 'We have a responsibility to ourselves and to the others. We need to go through every hiding place.'

'Good grief, doctor. You're a real stiff spine.'

'There's another set of stairs at the end of this floor. Perhaps we should continue down there?'

The stairs brought them down to a curio of a room; it was a ballroom and a little odd. The room, fifty feet square, was panelled fully ten feet high. Vertical windows rose above that so you could only look out to the slate roof tiles and beyond that to the clouds and stars. Light sconces cast in the shape of boughs held silken shades in their twig-like fingers.

'Why are the windows so high up?'

Cyrus had the solution. 'It's a private place,' he announced.

'Private?'

'Bloody servants everywhere. See and hear everything. Bloody creatures get under your feet.'

'It must be so hard to put up with,' said Quigg.

'Not here, though. Servants not allowed.' He pointed out a serving hatch disguised as part of the wall. 'See that? That's the dolly door—ring that bell, and they serve you through that. You can close it off, and no one can see you and no one can peek in from outside.' He put an arm around Eleanor's waist. She had no objection. 'We're safe from all eyes in here.'

'You mean to tell me,' Dr Quigg clarified, 'that this is a room for indecent activities?'

Cyrus howled. 'You devilish old prude! That's exactly what I'm saying, don't you know.' He pulled Eleanor close to his waist and quickly kissed her neck.

'Cyrus, really!' Eleanor protested, but her smile said quite another thing.

'There's a gallery up there, behind the curtain. There'll be a stair to it round the back.' He pointed it out, and indeed there was. 'Just enough room for a couple of musicians. They might have been blindfolded back in the day so they couldn't reveal what went on.' He pointed out a couple of chairs and a chaise longue against one wall. 'This is where you'd come to let your hair down, with no witnesses but whoever is in the room.' He spun Ms Grace around. 'A little foxtrot, a couple of martinis, and none of the servants to peek in the windows and no one around to judge.'

'Ta. Ta-da. Ta. Ta-da,' sang Eleanor to an imagined beat.

'What are you doing?' asked Quigg of Sir Cyrus, who had taken Miss Grace on a waltz.

'Masked balls. Costumed revelry. Can you imagine what went on? I'm dancing with the adorable Miss Grace, Dr Quigg! Madam, you dance very well.'

'Why, thank you! You are quite the soft-shoe yourself, handsome knight. Are you quite as accomplished at anything else?' She dropped a hand down onto his hip.

'Really, Sir Cyrus, Miss Grace, please! I think we should keep to our task.'

'I'd have you over the back of the chair,' Cyrus whispered into the widow's perfumed ear.

Miss Grace, three husbands behind her already, milked a crimson smile. 'Don't make promises you don't intend to keep.'

'My dear, I'll keep every promise to you.'

She laughed. 'Cyrus, you dear boy, tell me something.'

'Anything.' He had his lips at her neck.

'Those things that were read in the letter about you; tell me, were any of them true?'

'I might not have lived the life of a choir boy, but I carry a clean bill of health.'

'You're not telling lies, are you, Cyrus? It's…important. I want to know.'

'I'm as healthy and clean as a bull. Cross my heart.'

'What are the pair of you whispering about?' Dr Quigg called over.

'Not to worry, Doctor Quigg! Strategy for the week ahead.'

The mountain, Beinn Sted, was up on their left. A gradual slope rose up to her summit; no hint on this side of her sheer broken cliffs or of the thousand-foot plunge into the Atlantic. The Austin-Healey bumped along the track, which began its descent into the next bay. The road ended there— they had gone as far as they could without getting out and hiking.

The bay might be pretty, a postcard even, if it were not for their disquiet. Two squat houses sat in the valley, little bigger than sheds, their gable walls still supporting a chimney. They were ruins, their roofs long ago collapsed. Who had lived there, no one knew, and there was no one around to ask. There was no pier, no boat in sight, no rowing boat drawn up above the tide line. The surf broke over half-hidden rocks—it would be a perilous approach for the *Selkie*. The only thing of note was a small graveyard that stood a little ways off from the houses. Atop a grassy knoll, it was circled by a wall. Mortality by the ocean.

'Seems a little out of place?'

'A cemetery? I don't think so. You've got to be buried somewhere.'

The sanctified plot was fenced in stone, stacked up native rock. The grass within, a brilliant green, was shorn neat by the grazing of animals. Sheep had long ago found a route inside to confound the will of the wall. There were droppings, both fresh and old, and patches of wool hung like prayer flags where the beasts had rubbed against the stone. Tumbled headstones pitched and dipped, buffeted by the Atlantic gyre. The cemetery had one rusting gate last painted in antediluvian times.

'It appears that no one is home.'

The cemetery had a fine view to west and the Hebrides. Trailing islands were visible in the distance and onward, beyond that, the North Atlantic. New England over the horizon, Newfoundland along the way. The diaspora's last view. Yet this Christian scene of frugal impermanence—Thomas McLeod, 1782–1836, Master quarryman, who shared his sleep with his children, first Anne 1808–1809 14 months, then Donald 1809–1820, 11 yrs 3 months, and finally, after burying them all, his widow, her name unreadable—had been disturbed by more than the sheep. A mausoleum of Herculean marble upset the balance of the place.

'Who the hell is buried there?' barked DB. You could stand under it out of the rain.

'Lady Yvette Regette Valois-Black. Frenchy name, don't you think? So it says. 1832–1894. And Lady Monica bla-bla-bla hyphen Black, died in 1963,' Charlie read, skipping a few middle names. 'This is where the Black women go, apparently. Should we somehow care?'

'There's one more.'

And indeed there was. The lettering was still sharp and precise when the lichen and moss were rubbed off.

'Alexander George Black, Viscount Beitheach. I think we've found our Lord Black.'

'One of them, anyway. Maybe his granddad? Died in 1975.'

The tomb was large enough to fit a few people inside. 'Could someone hide in there?'

'Are you serious? What is this? No one's going to hide in a grave,' DB berated her, but the idea had been planted. 'Oh, come on!'

'How would you get a thing like this open?'

Charlie gave it his best, but it would not budge, at least not without a crow bar or lever.

'There's no sign of scratches. It's covered in moss.'

'Lichen.'

'What?'

'Doesn't matter.'

'The last one through this door was old Alex.'

'All right. But he didn't bring those flowers.'

There were flowers. They looked, at most, a week old.

'Perhaps the MacGregors brought them here?' Joan suggested. The men did not manage a reply. Someone had brought them, tied them in a little bow, and left them to wilt against the slab.

Charlie had a thought. 'They don't look like the sort of flowers you'd expect to find growing in a place like this. They're not local to the island, I mean.'

'Native to the glasshouses, do you think?' Joan's suggestion rang of sense.

'Another question for the staff,' DB said. 'We're collecting more questions than answers right now. None of this is getting any clearer.'

Charlie felt down. The day that had started with the excitement of the car had taken a turn for the glum. It was too open, too cold and windy, despite being summer, to imagine anyone living outdoors. Yet the slope of the hills, the bracken and heather, could give cover to a man lying low. The gorse of the stream bank would cover a body that might be watching them even now. Was someone there? Was Black out there with binoculars, enjoying himself? Was he some sort of survivalist nut? What sort of plan did he have? A man living rough would have to hunt like a beast, taking sheep or deer or fish. But he wasn't a man living rough. There was water everywhere, and he'd had plenty of time to lay in supplies if he'd wished. He might have a tent. Infrared goggles. An arctic suit for the cold nights. Black could really be anywhere, Charlie realised. The idea made him more depressed.

'I think you're right, Mr Bowers. What you said earlier. I don't think it likely we'll catch Black in a search.'

'Damn right.'

'We're going to have to lie in wait for him. Wait until Black comes to us,' said Charlie.

'Set a trap. We'll get him, or we'll escape.' The alternative went unsaid.

'Damn right we will.'

'Sooner or later, it's going to happen. Our host will have to show his hand.'

'Let's head on. Let's leave the car here and keep going,' Joan suggested, but the wind had gone out of the men. The flowers perhaps, or the weight of futility, or maybe the start of the rain.

'No. Let's stop at that cabin on the way back and take anything useful, just in case. But let's go back. We've spent too long doing this already.'

'Smartest thing you've said since breakfast, Charlie.' DB headed for the car.

Which was a shame, because if they had persevered on foot, then two headlands over they would have spied a sailboat in a cove, anchored with its sails drawn and wrapped. Whether it was tourists laid up or travellers off course or someone else with a private purpose, they were not to know or discover. The boat bobbed quietly on the swell, and no one appeared on deck. A week later it was gone, as if it had never been there.

⬭⬤⬤⬭

The doctor, the knight, and the actress of the screen went down to the baths, the last place they had been tasked to search. These lay at the bottom of the garden, before the golf course, through a tiled hall full of statuary. The baths were not built to fit in, for while Taigh Dubh was a fine old house pretending to be a castle (how else to explain the enormous windows, quite out of place in a neighbourly clan siege?), the baths pretended to be Roman—or was it Greek? Marble columns—*Ionic or Doric?* Cyrus could never remember— looked like a Las Vegas attraction. It was Olympian, built for Zeus's approval, and so well fashioned he must have been proud.

'Do you think those statues are real?'

'What is a real statue?'

'You know what I mean. Old.'

Dr Quigg could feel the moisture; it was the heat she wasn't expecting. 'Excuse me if I take off my coat.'

Like the greenhouses to the west of the house, the baths were thermally fed, an extravagance of engineering that brought the heat of the tropics to the place.

'It's freezing in my room. If I'd known this place was here last night, I'd have dragged my bed down here.'

There was a swimming pool, twenty yards across, and it billowed on the side nearest the house around a piece of re- markable sculpture—Triton, perhaps, or his father Poseidon. There were no fig leaves to disguise anatomy. There were mermaids at intervals spouting water foam and a jumble of horses with fish tails. The bottom of the pool was fin- ished with coloured tile whose pattern extended up the sides. Aegean blue and gold, it continued over the surround, a Celtic knot with no apparent end that wound back upon itself. It was a shameless mix of cultures both as ancient as the rocks. The cracks of taste were pasted over with money and bore the weight of purloined antiquity.

'You're incorrigible, Cyrus.' Eleanor removed his hand.

'How warm is the water, do you think?'

'It reminds me of Iceland or Yellowstone, only the smell there is a little strong.'

'And the surroundings are a little less gauche?'

'Fancy a swim?' asked Eleanor.

'Perhaps later, darling. Doctor, you're welcome as well.'

'I'm of the opinion that I'm a little less welcome with each minute we three spend together.'

No Black. No sign of Black here or anywhere they looked beyond their host's bedroom. Had they been more focused or canny, they might have asked why that was the case.

⊗⊗⊗⊗

'Any luck?'

'No. No boat. Nothing.'

'No sign of our illustrious host?'

'No. 'Fraid not. What's with the fancy car?'

'It's the only thing we came across. Well, apart from a couple of other things.'

The subject of the flowers caused much excitement. In the drawing room, with mutterings of renewed acquaintance, they shared what they had learned.

'Somebody put them there.' The statement was as obvious as the bouquet. Dr Quigg had seen that sort of flower growing in the greenhouse. Mrs MacGregor was asked, 'Did you deliver them?' She confessed she had not and asked the guests to believe that she had never seen anything of the island. 'I never heard of a cemetery there until you mentioned it just now.' And what had she been doing on the few days before they had arrived? 'Seeing to the house that needed getting readied.' Charlie Fotheringham said aside to Joan, 'A remarkable lack of curiosity.'

'Is your husband around, Mrs MacGregor? We're wondering if we might have a word.'

'You'll find him busy under the stairs.'

'Under the stairs?'

'He's been trying to get it going. The organ thing.'

'Whatever do you mean?'

The house had no stereo, no television, no satellite dish. There was a radio, a relic of the 70's of West German manufacture, with a dial that included long wave. Three D-cells might have coaxed it to life had it not lain undiscovered behind a rolling pin tucked at the back of a kitchen drawer. Taigh Dubh had not succumbed to an iPod player, but wasn't empty of the potential for sound; music, indeed, was built into its walls in the shape of the orchestrion.

'Goodness me,' Charlie exclaimed. 'What is it that's living under here?'

The orchestrion; a mechanical spectacular, a leviathan amongst musical boxes. Piping and pulleys, belts and bellows, rollers and gearing and springs. Much of the room following the slant of the stairs was filled with a church organ's pipes. A pair of legs kicking like a frog protruded from underneath.

'Mr MacGregor? Are you in there?' asked Charlie. A red metal toolbox sat propped open.

'Pass me the screwdriver, Mr Fotheringham? A number 2 Phillips. It's on top.'

Charlie obliged.

'I think I've got her,' said the Scot.

'Be careful in there. There's not much room.'

There was a blast of dust in the chord of C minor, and then the drawing room groaned to a Germanic beat.

'Extraordinary.'

'What the hell is that?'

Charlie helped Mr MacGregor out from under the belts and wheels. It sounded to him like a Munich beer hall, but the gillie looked very pleased.

'Beethoven, sir. There's different music on the different reels.'

'Do you think you can get it to play anything new?'

MacGregor said sourly that he did not.

'Do you mind coming into the drawing room a moment? We've a couple of things to ask you.'

MacGregor acquiesced.

'Have a seat, MacGregor.' Inspector Vail gave him his. 'What about a drink?'

MacGregor declined.

'We managed to make it up the island a bit. Have you been over the ground yourself?' Charlie was cordial.

'Of course, sir. I'm taken on as Lord Black's gillie, as I've made you all aware. I've seen some of it in this little time. It's my job to be familiar with his land.'

'And have you been to the game lodge, then? The one just up the glen?' Charlie asked. DB, Joan, and Inspector Vail looked on, waiting for what he would say.

MacGregor's face twisted. 'Aye, sir. I saw it two days ago. Place is a disgrace.'

'It wasn't you, then, Mr MacGregor, that laid out those beasts that way?' The loping head crowned in antlers. The belly open, nested with flies.

'No self-respecting gillie would have it like that, sir. I don't know what's the matter with the man who did it. Seems unnecessary and cruel.'

Didn't clean it up, though, Charlie thought.

'How long do you figure it had been like that?'

MacGregor seemed to think. 'Couple of weeks?' he volunteered. 'No more than a month?'

'And have your travels taken you as far as the small cemetery in the next bay over?'

'I've been there, aye. Lovely spot. Lonely in a way.'

'And that would have been when?'

'Two days. The same. Me and Mrs MacGregor have told you already—we've only been here these last three days.'

'And did you see the flowers, MacGregor?' Inspector Vail asked.

'Not that I can mind.'

'Do you think you *would* have seen them?' asked Joan.

'If they were as you described them, then maybe I would. What does it matter who it was? Someone put them there.'

'But not you.'

'No sir, not me.'

'Then someone else is out there.'

'If that is all the questions that you have, I need to be getting in wood from the shed.'

Ta-ta-ta-DA! The stairs shook to life as the belt made another loop. It was a mix of Thomas the Tank Engine playing loose with Beethoven's Fifth.

'You'd better take someone with you, MacGregor. No telling what's going to happen next.' Inspector Vail fixed the man with a stare.

'I'll come with you, Mr MacGregor,' Charlie volunteered. 'Safety in numbers, I guess.'

'When you were down there with your screwdriver, MacGregor, did you happen to see an off switch?'

◑◆◆◑

Later, when the daylight began to dull, the lights in the bathhouse were noticed.

'That's funny, I don't remember them being turned on when we were down there earlier.' It was Eleanor who drew their attention.

Cyrus couldn't remember either way, though Dr Quigg thought she was right.

'Has someone else been down there since we came back? Should we send Mr MacGregor to turn them off?'

'Where is MacGregor, anyway?'

'The fellow's been fixing that orchestrion thing. It was him making all that noise.'

'Well, he finished that some hours ago.'

'I heard Mrs MacGregor send him for wood.'

'Did somebody go with him?'

'I did,' said Charlie. 'We brought piles of the stuff back in.'

'MacGregor!' DB hailed, putting down his glass to look for a bell. 'Somebody ring for him.'

The diminutive Mrs MacGregor appeared.

'Get your husband, please.'

'I'm sorry, sir.' She looked around, concerned. 'I thought he was in here.'

In the end they all paid a visit to the baths. Fear sometimes works that way. No one really wanted to go, and yet no one wanted to stay. DB and Vail went first, side by side, leaving scarcely any room at all between their chests and the statues. Two by two they gambolled, an ape-like migration of worry. Charlie and Joan, Eleanor and Cyrus, Quigg with an arm around Mrs MacGregor. 'I'm sure he's all right dear. I'm sure.'

Dr Quigg's reassurance was short-lived.

MacGregor floated face down in the swimming pool, blood blossoming from out of his head.

'Don't look, dear. Don't look.'

The warm current that circulated night and day had carried MacGregor to Poseidon's feet. He looked, in turn, like a sacrifice or an observant saying his prayers. His coat and pants pulsed with the current, his arms stretched out like a supplicant sinner. But they were not fooled. This was no prank. The soupy discharge and unnatural buoyancy spoke of one result.

'We have found our gillie, and he has been murdered. This is no accident here.'

Mrs MacGregor looked and saw, and she wailed before she wept.

They snagged MacGregor's belt on the third attempt, reaching for it with a pole. None of them wanted to get into the pool and mix with the water and his blood. They dragged him to the side and hefted him out, and Dr Quigg examined the body. 'Blunt force trauma,' she said, touching MacGregor's scalp.

'What does that mean?' Charlie asked.

Inspector Vail answered for her. 'Fellow's been hit on the head. Hit on the head and then dumped.'

There was a bump where the scalp had been split. The wound leaked and marred the tile, which was smeared in a black cherry red.

'He's warm!' Charlie said. He'd straightened out MacGregor's arms.

Dr Quigg quickly dispelled that hope. 'It's only the water he was in.' She double-checked for a pulse just in case, but even now he was growing cold.

'Robert! No, Robert!' sobbed his wife.

'Please help her. Somebody. Take her back to the house,' Joan asked, but no one was listening, and Mrs MacGregor would not go.

'What are we going to do with the corpse?' Cyrus stroked his chin.

'Don't call him that,' said Joan.

'What else *should* we call him?' Eleanor sounded amused.

'The police won't want him moved,' said Charlie.

'Bugger the police. There's no-one is here. Today should have told you that,' said Cyrus.

'Then do we leave him?' asked the doctor.

'Bring him up to the house. Carry him back. Let's do that at least,' said DB.

'The investigators are not going to be happy,' cautioned Charlie.

'If you say that again, I believe I will hit you.' They weren't sure if Cyrus was being sincere.

'Please! Enough. All right, then, let's bring him with us. There's nothing else here we can do.' The doctor made the decision for them.

Before lifting MacGregor, Charlie draped him with a bath towel of white and Aegean blue, which clung to him as it grew damp. 'I don't like him looking at me,' he explained.

Mrs MacGregor held her dead husband's hand until Ms Hedringer led her away.

'There's an empty room beside Sterling's,' DB suggested. Having trouble with his leg, he had scouted the room as an alternate to the one he was in. 'Maybe we can put him there?' It sounded like a good idea; or at least, no one suggested anything else.

The men lifted up the body. It slumped in an unfortunate way.

It was a predatory darkness when it came, darker tonight for the rain and worse for another discovery. They had only finished laying MacGregor down when Cyrus noticed the change.

'Look at the fireplace,' he told them.

There had been nine green bottles—they had been looked at innumerable times. But now there were only eight. Each had been spaced evenly out, which made counting them all the easier.

Chapter 7
A Noise in the Night

EIGHT GREEN BOTTLES. HOWEVER MANY TIMES THEY COUNTED them, they only came up with eight. One was gone, and MacGregor with it—it was nowhere to be seen. Cyrus tapped his whisky glass against each remaining one. *Ting, ting, ting.*

'Please stop.'

'Lord Black came in and took a bottle from here. Doesn't that seem strange to you?' Cyrus asked. 'He obviously risked being seen.'

They had all gathered in the drawing room in front of the enormous fireplace. Above the mantelpiece, on the wall, Lady Monica Black looked down on them from a portrait of her on a horse. *She* had witnessed the re-arrangement of bottles, but what she had seen, she refused to share.

'We were all out,' DB answered. 'There's no mystery here. We were all down at that swimming pool, and Black had all the time he needed.'

'Were we?' Cyrus replied. 'How could he be sure? Was he watching us?' He chewed the idea like a dog with a bone, unwilling to give it up.

Inspector Vail backed up Cyrus's doubts. 'Pretty cocky doing that. Not knowing if any one of us would turn back and find him. Hell of a risk he was taking.'

'Then we were lucky that no one did!' Charlie was wiping his glasses, which kept fogging up. 'Anyone who came back and saw him would have ended up dead too.'

'Maybe,' said Inspector Vail. For a brief moment what might have been contempt was written on his face. 'But there was still a chance an alarm could be raised. Gordon's got a point.'

'Why did he go out alone?' Eleanor asked from the couch.

'Who? Black?'

'No, of course not. Mr MacGregor. Why did Mr MacGregor go alone?'

'Do we have to talk about this right now?' Joan took great offense. She had sheltered Mrs MacGregor back up to the house and stood guard over her now. *Let me stay with Robert*, the tiny woman had asked as they lay the wet body in the room, but the group had refused to leave her alone and insisted she return with them. The poor woman was shaking, fists clenched, hugging herself. 'Drink something,' Joan had said to her, 'It will help to make you feel better.'

'Honey,' said Eleanor, 'the man's dead. I feel bad, I really do, but I'm kind of invested in how it all happened. You'd have to be nuts to go out by yourself. Why do you think he went down here like that?'

'Who says he went alone?' the inspector put in.

'Is the wood shed nearby?'

'No. It's on the other side of the house,' confirmed Charlie, his clothes still smelling of pine.

'Perhaps he went there to meet someone,' suggested the inspector. 'Somewhere out of the way?'

'Perhaps he fancied a couple of laps before sitting down to mend a hole in his kilt?' Cyrus had no time for this game. Whatever his reason for going to the bathhouse, MacGregor wasn't telling them.

Eleanor, at least, found it funny. 'Bagpipe practice!'

It was the doctor's turn to take umbrage at the actress. 'That is in very poor taste.'

DB had mixed Eleanor another drink, and the media mogul passed her the glass, taking the empty one back from her hand. He'd yet to hear her say 'no.'

'Let's back it up,' said Inspector Vail. 'One thing at a time. Everyone was in the big house, weren't we?' He was trying to place them all at the scene.

'Black was watching us, and when we went out, he snuck in here and stole a bottle away,' was the doctor's assessment.

The room sank into a silence, which let the little sounds of the house grow bold; the persistent patter of a wind thrown rain at an angle against the glass, the hiss and snap of a sap rich log that fizzed within the heat of the fire, the throaty tune from the watt-variable bulbs that dimmed and then hummed to a glow. Charlie saw the lights and thought of an army of mice harnessed to run in a wheel. *Black was watching us…* he was out there. Was he watching them still?

Everyone felt it, DB was sure, and he told himself he wasn't afraid. He'd been in a few tough spots in his time, as he kept reminding himself. DB didn't put his success down to luck, oh no, he wasn't the sort to sit by. His first thought when he'd seen the floating Scotsman was where the old guy had stashed his gun. In the mêlée of bringing MacGregor to his room, he had tested his suspicion and won. The game-keeper's shotgun—the only accessible gun on the island as far as he knew—had been in the room under the man's own bed! DB grinned to himself. It was a piece of work well done, he thought, congratulating himself. Wave the walking stick, play it up, and rub the leg as if the pain throbs sore. Claim a seat on the edge of the bed because you are lame and they are strong. Let the others work and talk. Let them think they're in control. Let my nurse help the shattered widow, everyone migrating towards a drink, happy to be out of that room. Off they had gone. Sore leg, sore. *I'll just be along in a minute.* As soon as they were down the hall, move the gun back to my own room.

DB threw back another Scotch. It was hidden now under his own mattress—comforting to know. Let that bastard

Black come for him tonight! He'd be in for a big surprise. 'What are you saying, what's all this talk heading to?' The others in the room were starting to talk around him, and for DB that would not do. 'If you've got something to say, say it up front. Don't mumble, boy. Spit it out!'

'Let's just put things straight.' Cyrus paced back and forth in front of the fireplace where he'd discovered a green bottle was missing. He mulled his words before he spoke, and those gathered leaned in close. 'I think it might help all of us to retrace our steps. I want to go through how we all got here and get a clear picture of what we all know.'

'What the hell's the point of all that?' DB bristled. 'There's a madman out there with some agenda, and he ain't a fan of us.'

'It might help you get out alive, Mr Bowers,' Inspector Vail pointed out.

'Let him talk, please! Let him go on. DB, you'll have your chance.' Charlie wanted to hear.

Cyrus checked his mobile phone for the time. 12% battery remaining. He put one hand on the mantle. 'Things...' he started, 'I'm starting to believe,' he qualified, 'are not entirely as they seem.'

'I hope you've got more than that.' Dr Quigg had that twist in her mouth.

Cyrus ignored her. He went on. 'Let's start with the letter.'

'Not that again.'

'But, my large American friend, it is the source, the reason for our invitation.'

'I was invited here to buy an island,' DB repeated.

'No, sir, you were not.'

DB wasn't used to being told he was wrong. 'You'd better explain yourself, Gordon. What are you talking about?'

'Please pipe down and let the man talk!' Joan had had quite enough.

'Thank you, Ms Hedringer. I'll try and be clear. As I was saying, it just isn't adding up.' He tapped the green bottles again. 'Let me tell you what's in my head, and then the rest of you can fill in the gaps.

'I thought, on the boat over, that we were a motley crew. Black had assembled a strange lot. It wasn't your usual demographic up for a week of sport. Please don't take offense—I noticed Mr Sterling disembark from a bus. He was carrying cheap luggage, some sort of nasty fake leather, and he didn't know where he was going. And his clothes—his well worn coat, and that university scarf in need of a wash. I saw a man clinging to old glories and likely not a local. A man short of a few pounds. He stuck out like a sore thumb. I watched him from the conservatory window in the dining room of my little hotel. That was what I thought of him before I realised he was coming with us. I've been at a few of these social gatherings over the years, and fellows off a bus aren't...well, they're not the sort you expect to see.'

'So what? So his wife's got the car. You're jumping to conclusions, Gordon. And what does it matter now anyway?'

'Please, let me continue. So I asked myself, 'What is Black up to?' That was what I wondered on the boat. My first thoughts were less than flattering, but my nose for the odd was not wrong. What I didn't appreciate until it was too late was that it wasn't just Sterling who was wrong. It wasn't just him out of place—no, not just poor old Sterling—it was every one of us.'

There was a silence in the drawing room, the sound of eight people trying to figure out whether they'd just been insulted or not.

Cyrus jumped ahead of them. 'You see, we don't belong. Individually, yes. The trap was baited with plausibility, each appealing to one's own vanity. But together? No. I'm sure you are all lovely people, but we're oil and water when mixed. Black brought us here with a purpose. We were lured, if you don't know it already. Deceived. This is a trap, and he has sprung it.'

'Lured?'

'What do you mean, 'a trap'?'

'Isn't it obvious? I had thought, hearing the letter being read on the first night, that Black was having a good joke. I now believe that everything in that letter was true, every word of it. I believe that each of us is guilty as charged, just as MacGregor read out. Let me tell you that the Black I knew was a man of his word—is a man of his word. He means to do for us all.'

'But I haven't killed a damn soul!' DB pledged.

'No?' Cyrus seemed wryly amused. 'Your papers don't denigrate opponents? You never backed the call for war?'

'I never pulled a trigger on anyone, but don't think I won't start soon!'

'Mr Bowers, please calm down.'

He was red in the face. 'Anyone who gets between me and getting off this rock had better watch out!'

Inspector Vail was tight with impatience and trying to cover it up. He said to Cyrus, 'Forgive me for asking, but is there anything you've established that might be described as *new*? There are two dead bodies that tell us exactly what you're saying—none of this is what we had planned.'

Cyrus fingered his glass again, looking them up and down. *Unruly-haired Charles Fotheringham, Black's biographer, no money there; the tidy Joan Hedringer, Bowers' nurse, who hadn't been invited along; the widow Mrs...was it Wanda? No. Wendy MacGregor, who makes a terrible soup; the horse-faced Dr Frances Quigg, a pin forever in her arse; the supine Eleanor Grace, may her name forever glow in the stars and her garters always snap; angry ex-Inspector Henry Vail, who looks like he needs to hit something very soon, I'd rather it wasn't me; fat and fortified DeeBee Bowers III, where does he stash all his loot? And our absentees; Andrew Sterling, if that was really his name; wet Mr MacGregor; and our host.*

Cyrus took that minute, during which he scribed the memory of their faces on his mind. 'I think one of you is helping Black. I think one of you is working with him, and is here to set us up. One of you helped kill Andrew and MacGregor. One of you is in on it.'

'What's that?'

'Ridiculous!'

Faces full of bluster, suspicion, fear… but did Cyrus see anything like guilt? Some of them wouldn't meet his eye, and others were steaming red. Eleanor raised her heavy crystal glass and gave him an encouraging wink.

'I don't trust any one of you,' he continued. 'But until we figure out which one of you it is, more of us are going to die.'

'Do you really mean what you're saying?'

'I tell you, someone in this room took the bottle when we went to the bathhouse tonight.'

'Surely that was Black?'

'I don't think so. I think one of you is in on it.'

'That's a hefty accusation to make!' DB challenged him.

'The ferry arrives on Friday. There's plenty of food, but no boat until then. This plan was a long time in the making.'

'Then what do you suggest we should do?' demanded Quigg.

'Partner up. Don't trust anyone. Keep each other safe until we're rescued.'

Inspector Vail was more sarcastic, or maybe he had started to crack. 'Take MacGregor's lead and go for a swim. Anyone for a game of pool?'

⊙⊗⊗⊙

'We'll make a radio.'

'Do you know how to make a radio?'

'No. Do you?'

'No. Do you know what parts you need to make a radio?'

'No. Not the faintest idea. A lot of wire and springs and dials and all that sort of thing. I imagine that's how it goes. And you'll need a good box to hold everything in.'

'I suspect you're right. Not much hope for a radio, then.'

'No, I imagine not.'

'Pity.'

'What about your mobile?'

'What about it?'

'Doesn't it do radio too?'

'Internet radio.'

'Oh.'

'Yes, quite a shame, that. I know what you mean. I had hopes for a radio with a dial. One of those marine radios that you call *Mayday* on.'

'With a dial, yes. We could have called the authorities. Got the Coastguard out.'

'No radio, though.'

'No, I think not. Do they still have *Mayday*, now that I think of it? Or did they give that up?'

'I'm sure it would be worth a try. Here's a thought, though. What about flags instead?'

'Flags?'

'Yes, you know—coloured flags, like those sailor fellows used to wave about. Tell someone we need help.'

'Do you have any flags about you?'

'No, I haven't seen any flags. But you've got to admit they would be a whole lot easier to make than a radio would.'

'I suspect so. Do you know what the flags mean?'

'Haven't a clue. How big do you think a flag would have to be to see it all the way from the coast?'

'That's a big flag you're talking about. And we would need a big pole to hang it from.'

'Do we have a big flag pole, do you think?'

'There's a little blighter, on the roof upstairs. Above the front doors. Flying the saltire and the Union flag.'

'Covering his bases.'

'Would that work?'

'The flags?'

'No, the flagpole.'

'Useless, I would think. Far too small for our job. You can barely see it from down by the bathhouse, never mind the mainland.'

'Anything bigger than that, then?'

'Not that I've seen.'

'No?'

'Can't be too hard to make, though. A flag pole, don't you think?'

'Or we could lay the flags out on the ground. One of those airplanes might see it if they tear about overtop.'

'We could try that. Or make a flagpole.'

'You're stuck on that flagpole idea.'

'Must be easy to make. I'm sure we could cobble one of those.'

'We'll need a big sodding tree, like they have in California. Enormous trees they have in America. I saw a documentary once.'

'Are there any Californian trees about here? The island seems a little short on trees in general, actually. A few little Christmas tree ones, that's all I've seen.'

'Not a lot of big buggers, no. Up the glen there were quite a few, but how would you get them down?'

'Heavy blighters too, I imagine.'

'Bit of a problem there.'

'Now you mention it.'

'Pity that. Flags was a good idea.'

'Not bad. Could have worked, except for that bit about a tree for the pole.'

'And having no flags, don't forget.'

'As you say. The flag bit.'

'What about hot air balloons?'

'Hot air balloons?'

'Yeah, what about them?'

'Do you think they'll send hot air balloons?'

'No. Making them, I mean. I'm not even sure that boat is coming back. Black probably sent that fellow a letter telling him the plans had changed.'

'Probably phoned him on his satellite phone from his secret lair with the jacuzzi and fridge. 'Dear Captain Birdseye, take the rest of the month off.' Something like that he sent. Probably paid him a bonus too.'

'Likely.'

'Do you think the *Selkie*'s not coming then? No one will show up on Friday?'

'Even if it does show up, it's still a wait. How hard do you think a balloon is to make?'

'A hot air balloon? Got to be easy. You just need a balloon, and a fire to heat the air. Hot air and a balloon—not a lot other than that. You could make lots of hot air to fill it up if you had a fire. And then you'd need the wind from the proper direction.'

'You ever made a hot air balloon?'

'No. Never.'

'Pity.'

'Yes. Never had the need before now.'

Another minute passed, as minutes do when making hours.

'There's that network signal again. Someone close has got an iPhone on.'

'Oh, yeah?'

'Yeah. Do you have a charger that works? The plugs in this house are a bit off.'

'No, sorry. Mine doesn't work either. We should try and save the battery that's left.'

'Should have brought a solar charger.'

'That would have been smart.'

'Pity.'

'Pity. Yeah.'

'Say, I had another thought. Have you ever made a yacht? Sails and things. Doesn't need to be that big, you know. What would you need for one of those?'

CONSTANT

'When I die, I want it to be in a stream of musket balls. A fog of gunshot across a morning plain.' DB parted the air with a slow moving hand, drawing the scene out for them.

'What bloody century are you living in, Bowers? Have you got some sort of Civil War fixation?' Cyrus wanted to know.

'Not a lingering wound—I'm not talking gangrene or amputation. I was thinking of a clean shot somewhere near my heart after a courageous charge to win the day.' He was getting glossy-eyed.

'And then what? You'll have some flunky write the obituary up and put it at the top of the news?'

'He can't do that. He'd be dead,' Eleanor pointed out.

'Wait a minute. Are you one of those nuts that dresses up in uniforms? Is that what you do on your weekends?' Cyrus asked.

'Will there be a sweetheart crying over your coffin, Mr Bowers?' Eleanor wanted to know.

It was getting late. The dim pulsing glow from the electric sconces chased the shadows and then let them back in. The party was gathered downstairs in the drawing room, which had become their refuge of choice—being able to see all the doors and passages had taken on a new degree of importance. The guests herded while passing the time, whether they were conscious of it or not.

Dr Quigg was playing cards at a green baize table. She dealt a variant of solitaire that had her win every hand; Ms Hedringer was trying to figure out the rules while pretending to read a book. 'The boys,' as they had become—Cyrus and Inspector Vail—drank and talked before the fire, sharing a laugh with Miss Grace. DB re-read his newspaper, three days old by now, snapping the pages with as much enthusiasm as he had the first time through. Mr Fotheringham had a notebook out and was gnawing on a pencil, seemingly its only purpose. Mrs MacGregor, poor woman, understandably seemed at a loss. She made tea, escorted of course, and brought a plate of meat pies from the pantry for devouring—it was the sum of their dinner for the day. After tidying everything away, she sat as far off as she could, toes turned pigeon in. There she lingered, hands in her lap, present and yet not quite with them. What could they say to her, poor woman, Mr MacGregor drowned and dead? So no one tried.

The musket ball conversation originated with the trio by the fire. The subject, apropos but in questionable taste, was 'How do you see yourself going?' To the participants it lightened the mood of the evening better than the wall lights were managing.

'Now Deebee,' the name had started with Cyrus but had spread to common use, 'let's be perfectly clear. If you only get to choose one way to die, this is how you will go?'

DB took aim along his arm and pulled the imagined trigger. 'Bang.'

'But is it a *stream* of musket balls we're talking, or just one clean shot that ends the day? I mean, a sodding stream is all about *pichow, piching, kabow!* Hot lead blasting you rotten. Bits flying everywhere. A different way to go entirely.' Cyrus collapsed across the couch, feigning Gettysburg slaughter.

'Oh, Cyrus!' Eleanor howled in glee, squashed beneath his acting.

Cyrus jumped back up. 'While a single shot is a lot more 'minute to find your girl's special letter' and read it before you expire.'

'What's in the letter? What's in the letter?' Eleanor demanded to know.

'She's heavy with child?' guessed Vail.

'She's running off with his best friend!' suggested a mischievous Miss Grace.

'She's just found out they're brother and sister, and mother says their love is wrong,' Frances Quigg chimed in.

'Oooh! Doctor! Wash the picture out of my head. Quite the imagination you've got,' Cyrus said approvingly.

'She'll love him forever, or until he's dead, or at least until a better one comes around. She's a practical girl and puts it nicely,' stated Inspector Vail, laying out the evidence.

'You're all terrible. They're terrible, Deebee, don't listen to any of them. I think she'll wait for you in the second life and mourn you all her days.' Eleanor was sympathetic.

'Deebee's the one that's dying,' corrected Cyrus unnecessarily.

'I tell you it's my death! I'm telling you musket balls, a volley of them, but there's only the one that lays me low.' He took another drink.

'A hero's death!' Cyrus toasted him.

'Now you're talking! They can bury me wrapped in the flag.'

'What about you, Gordon? How do you go?' It was DB who returned the favour.

'Me? Well, yes. We all have to go sometime. I suppose we should give it a thought. Whatever it is, however I go, it is *not* withering away in a home. No peeing my pants and forgetting my name. No doddering around being a nuisance. No heirs hanging around for my purse.'

'Then how does it end?' asked Eleanor Grace, her voice now soft and wet. Her arms were draped across the back of the couch. 'How does the great man fall low?'

'It's face to face; it's life or death. A fight with axes or swords.'

'You're worse than he is. Things have gone medieval now!' The inspector was keeping score.

'On the battlements?' Eleanor asked.

'No, in here. In this room.'

'In here?' The mood calmed down. The room grew colder.

'Yes. I see it coming and try to defend myself, but the blow is too strong for my parry. I see the axe head bearing down and then it smashes into me. I feel my bones shatter; I lose the use of my hand. I feel wet, like I've gone and pissed myself, and then I notice all the blood.'

'Oh, Cyrus, please don't!' Eleanor looked shocked, their sanctuary punctured.

'I fall to my knees. Right there.' He pointed to the rug. 'And then the villain pulls the axe out and leaves me bleeding.'

'Who is it? Who is it?'

'He doesn't smile or say anything. He just turns and

walks quietly out.'

The room went deathly silent. The shadows had grown brave and stretched out.

'Look at your faces!' Cyrus howled, laughing like a jackal or fool.

'That's not bloody funny!' DB was put out, but 'the boys' and Miss Grace thought it a hoot. More drinks were poured. They sang songs. Mr Fotheringham continued to take notes, Ms Hedringer went back to her book, and Dr Quigg won another hand.

⬤⬤⬤

Inspector Vail always locked his door. He always double-checked it. Tonight he checked it three times.

⬤⬤⬤

Eleanor Grace, snug in her sheets, could see Lady Monica's clock face through the northern twilight dark. With only the one hand—the hour hand on it—minutes had no meaning, and time moved slower for that. Eleanor Grace, snug in her sheets, admitted to herself she was scared—the furniture she'd stacked behind her door gave scant reassurance. Cyrus, disturbed by her agitation, woke up and put a warm arm around her breast.

'What's the matter, dear girl?'

'He's going to come for us all, Cyrus. Black's going to come for us all.'

'I suspect so, but not tonight, surely. Try and get some rest.'

'How can you be so sure?'

'There's a long game going on, darling. He likes his theatre, does Black. He could have poisoned us all the first day we were here, but instead he goes in for this. The bugger's been reading too many books. I'm certain he's gone off his head. No, there's a long game at play here, and I'm betting we are going to win. Don't you worry about poor old Black. Tomorrow we'll get him for sure.'

'You promise?'

'Come here, you luscious creature. I would never lie to you.' There was no more talk. The drama had him all stirred.

CRXXXD

'Come share a room with me, dear.' Dr Quigg tried to help, but Mrs MacGregor would not leave her husband. 'You can't stay here all night.'

Mrs MacGregor didn't speak, didn't argue, didn't reply, and showed no hint of complying. Of what private grief or thoughts consumed her she did not give any hint. She withdrew. Mrs MacGregor lay on the bed, her husband beside her on the floor.

Dr Quigg gave up. 'If I leave, you will you lock the door, Mrs MacGregor? Will you lock yourself inside? Be safe?' Getting no final acknowledgement, Dr Quigg turned and left.

Joan was waiting outside in the hall. 'Will she be all right?'

Dr Quigg had seen her share of trauma patients, but she did not know and said as much. 'It's always hard to predict how a loved one will react. We're all different, Ms Hedringer, in how we cope.'

'We can't leave her like this,' Joan said.

'Then what might you suggest?' Dr Quigg was short with the young woman; but indeed, what *was* there that anyone could do?

Joan opened the door. Mrs MacGregor's back was turned, and she lay curled up facing the wall.

'We're going to lock the door for you, Mrs MacGregor. The key will be on the floor.'

Joan took the key out of the inside of the lock and closed the door again. She locked the door, tested it, and then, the gap underneath allowing for it, slid the key violently back.

'I feel safer this way,' she told the doctor.

'And does she?'

Poor Mrs MacGregor. She's had a hard life. You can always tell.

CRXXD

Inspector Vail woke up. He almost knocked his loaded revolver out of its resting place in his lap as he got up out of the chair in the corner. The pillows he'd stuffed under his blankets looked like someone was asleep in his bed. He parted the curtains and looked outside. He had a pocket watch—a chronometer, a gift from a client—that informed him he'd dozed off for two hours. He'd taken the precaution of turning his phone off; his charger didn't work in these sockets. A light was on in an upstairs room across the courtyard from his own. It took a moment for Inspector Vail to realize that it came from Black's own room. Inspector Vail lifted his gun and, as quietly as he possibly could, opened the door to the corridor.

CRXXD

Joan Hedringer had taken an age to doze off. Every groan and creak in the old house was full of malcontent.

She awoke. She thought she heard a noise. She sat listening, craning her ear to the dark. Outside, something or someone was moving about. Someone was in the corridors.

CRXXD

Charlie jumped straight out of bed.

Knock, knock.

There it was again.

He fumbled for the iron poker he'd removed from the

fireplace earlier. Clutching it two-handed before him, he moved, bare footed, to the summons.

'Who's there?' he whispered, tensing his shoulders, ready for a swing.

'Mr Fotheringham, please open up. There's someone creeping about upstairs.'

It was Ms Hedringer's voice. Charlie turned the key and let her in.

She was in a state.

'There, there,' he comforted her, lowering the poker. She was shaking. He gave her the blanket he'd been using.

'There's someone up there. Up there now. I heard them sneaking around.' All this was relayed in whispers.

'Follow me,' he said, handing her the tongs. They were going to find out together.

Charlie went first, asking for silence with a finger on his lips, leading them, poker held up.

There was a surrealism to their sortie. Joan was warmer for the blanket around her shoulders but wondered if she should have left it behind. The tongs were heavy in her hand, and what was she expected to do with them? They went like thieves down the hall to the back stairs, the closest to the landing above. On the next floor, they edged closer to the noise and heard the squeaking of hinges on a door.

'Move an inch and I'll shoot you dead.' They weren't as silent as they had hoped.

'Inspector Vail?'

'Mr Fotheringham. And Ms Hedringer. Out for a spot of skulduggery?' He did not lower the heavy gun.

'Ms Hedringer heard a noise. We came up to investigate.'

Inspector Vail turned his head and looked up the passage behind them. 'You planning on stirring a fire with that thing?'

'It isn't loaded, if that's what you mean.'

Inspector Vail lowered the gun. 'Come have a look at this. Someone's been here fir.'

It was the same little bedroom, well proportioned, conservatively furnished, the same writing desk and pens and pots that they'd seen the day before. Only someone had been there since. The light was on, a desk oil lamp, and a burned-down match lay in the tray.

'I saw the light from my room.'

'There was no one here when you arrived?'

'No. It was just like this. Then you pair showed up.'

The bed was not disturbed, unslept in, but someone had been working at the desk. There was another drawing. It was the same paper, the same ink, the same penmanship as Sterling's cartoon, only this one was more recent.

It showed a rat figure, submerged, stuck in a bottle, a trident clasped in one drowned hand.

B is for Bob, a misnomer if any. The same blotchy brushstrokes.

B is for Bob
a misnomer if any.

'What was Mr MacGregor's first name?' asked the Inspector, although he already knew.

'Robert, I believe.'

Robert. Bob. He was playing with them. *B is for Bob. A is for Andrew, a paper-cut opener.*

'He's knocking us off alphabetically?'

Inspector Vail put his revolver away inside his overcoat. 'Take care, Mr Fotheringham—Charlie. Look after yourself.'

'It sounds improper, I'm sure it does, Mr Fotheringham, but I'm scared to go back to my room.'

Charlie didn't make any objections. Truth be told, he was glad of the company; the cartoon had given him the willies. Hours before he'd been sleeping unawares, while above him Black was making drawings. The lock on the door and the poker under the bed were not lending the invulnerability they once had.

'I'll take the couch,' she offered.

'No, I'll take the couch.' Charlie insisted, as a gentleman should. He heard her drift off to sleep.

The couch didn't prove very comfortable. It didn't matter. He didn't plan on sleeping, and for a long time he had his wish.

Frances lifted the coat hanger from the back of her door, and when she did so, it knocked her straw hat. *Bother*, she thought, watching it fall and roll, cartwheel across the room until it finally came to a rest. When had she started to feel old? But she did. Frances felt it in her knee and in her shoulder as she stretched to pick it up. She brushed off the hat and laid it flat on the dresser—it didn't look too worse for wear. She hung her dress to keep it from wrinkling, stepped from her shift into her flannel nightgown, and returned to the dressing table. Twenty strokes she gave her hair with her boar bristle hairbrush, then twenty more to the other side. The picture frame beside the straw hat carried a photograph of two young girls, and though the hair of one was black, not grey, it was recognizable still. Frances finished. Her shoes for tomorrow were laid out by the window beside the chair that carried her outfit. She had brushed her teeth already. She cast an eye at her doctor's bag and then over at the locked door. She stood uncertain for a moment, and then reached out one trembling hand. Gently the frame was tilted forward until the two young girls were hidden.

Chapter 8
Problem Plumbing

CHARLIE AWOKE. HIS MUSCLES OBJECTED, BENT OUT OF shape as they were. The sun was up and the curtains open. Joan was not in the bed. Charlie heard the water running and a woman's voice humming a melody from the bathroom next door. He heard the water turn off, then the *splish splash* of Joan getting into the tub, and he couldn't help but imagine her naked. The indulgence didn't last for a minute before the curious noise began. It started as a low-throat groan, like air trapped in the pipes. Joan's song slowed and stalled. Something was wrong. Charlie heard a snap from the bathroom, the sound of slapping water, and the very next moment Joan screamed.

Kar, kar, kar! The noise broke and shuddered, it jarred like the forcing of mismatched gears, like their drive in the car up the island. Charlie ran to the door. *Kar, kar, kar!* The foundry percussion stamped, a clockwork noise of iron. 'No. No!' he heard Joan scream, her panic audible amid the splashing and that ceaseless unnatural noise. *Kar, kar, kar!* Charlie tried the door, but it was locked from the inside.

'Joan! Joan!' He hit the door to break it. *Kar, kar!* He hit it again. It was a grinding of mechanical steel that reminded him of tank wheels in sand. Charlie shouldered the door a third time, falling into the bathroom as it opened. He couldn't make sense of what he saw.

Joan was in the bath, writhing and thrashing, but the bathtub was eating her up. There was Joan's arm, a breast, a leg sticking out, and the shower cabinet tilted down. It was wrong—it shouldn't look like that, a person under all of those pipes. The bath cabinet was folding in half, and Joan was under it all. *Kar, kar, kar!* Water was spilling over the tiled floor.

'Charlie!' Joan screamed, and then was cut off with a gurgle. Her pale arm flapped like a gull's broken wing dangling over the rim of the bath. The cabinet bore down like a clockwork press, a weight on flesh and bone, and a frantic Joan, a struggling Joan, was pinned and being pressed beneath it. Brass and copper tubing descended. Joan was being crushed while the ruptured plumbing filled the tub to above her head.

Charlie did not dither. Charlie did not dwell. He tore off the iron towel rack and wedged it into the infernal machine. At least for now the terrible pressure was arrested from driving Joan further down. Charlie laid into the bar and heaved with all his might. Joan's nails dug into his arm, her head held under the water. He leveraged the railing and pried the cabinet up, and Joan, frantic Joan, took a breath.

'Get out! Climb out!' he ordered her. He put all his weight into it. If the bar gave in or broke off now, then she was surely done for. Joan slithered naked, turned like an eel, and squeezed through a gap to the floor.

Charlie let go of the bar. The shower stall fell flat with jarring pressure, and the tub water sloshed and spilled over. Seconds more and Joan would have been caught, trapped with no way out—if not drowned, then broken to pieces. Joan spluttered and coughed as she lay curled on the tiles amidst a puddle of spreading water. Charlie bent over, hands on knees. The enormity of what had happened made him dizzy.

'Are you all right?' he asked her, humbly.

'You saved me, Charlie. You did.'

Charlie went to a shelf of towels and handed her a few. Joan was crying. He was embarrassed. 'I can't promise I won't peek.'

'What was it? What happened? Why did it do that, Charlie?'

But Charlie couldn't provide an answer.

'Do you think it was Black?' She held tight to him as he watched the water spill on out through the door. 'But no one else was in the room. No one else but you.'

She still held onto him, but he felt it now—an awkwardness in the situation. 'Are you sure you're okay? Here, let me get you up. We'll get you some dry clothes.'

Could it have been set up before? Charlie wondered, but then if so, had it been meant for him? *C for Charlie,* and not meant for Joan at all?

'You know, Joan, maybe this is just a coincidence. Old house. Old plumbing. I don't know. The alternative is hard to consider.'

'You don't need to say anything. I didn't mean to sound suspicious. If it wasn't for you, Charlie, I'd be gone.'

∞⊗∞

It was a muted breakfast.

The good of it, for those in search of such omens, was that Mrs MacGregor was back amongst them. She was up before any of them, scrubbing and sweeping with a singular purpose, burning sausages and cooking oatmeal. But she did not talk, nor did she meet their eye. Something in her had changed. She moved head bowed, wringing her hands when they were not full or occupied. Nor, it was soon apparent, did she attend to any of the duties that Mr MacGregor had seen to before. The fires were not set, for it was Mr MacGregor who had brought the wood for that and saw to their timely combustion. The fires being unlit, despite the month, the house suffered with a chill.

Of more pressing interest was the state of the plumb-

ing. It would have been Mr MacGregor they called upon to
mend the disturbed pipes. Everyone with the exception of
Mrs MacGregor came to see Charlie's room.

'Extraordinary!'

'Do you think it was an accident?'

'It's lucky she got out alive.'

There were more than a few looks exchanged. What,
some wondered, was the naked Ms Hedringer doing in Mr
Fotheringham's rooms? A stuttering explanation from the
blushing Fotheringham didn't go far to convince any doubt-
ers.

Inspector Vail shared with the group his discovery of
the second drawing. *B is for Bob, a misnomer if any,* and he
propped the cartoon up on the mantel.

'They came up together.' He told of Joan and Charlie
and finding them in the corridor.

'And why,' DB challenged the Inspector, 'did you come
here with a gun?'

'I'm a cautious man.' Inspector Vail stared him down.
'If I had a second one with me and offered to share, are you
saying that you would decline?' He was now wearing the
revolver openly, and the brutish functionality of the thing
was a warning and threat to all.

The disappearance of the gamekeeper's shotgun had
reaffirmed the need for protection. They had discovered
it missing after the argument around the green bottles the
night before.

'And you are sure he always kept it here, Mrs MacGregor?'

'Leave the poor woman alone, Inspector! Hasn't she
been through enough?'

The oatmeal was thick and clumped like glue.

'Isn't there any more milk?' There was not. They drank
their coffee black.

'Well, you got lucky, Mr Fotheringham.' DB complimented. 'I suspect that bath was meant for you. A is for Andrew,
B is for Bob, C is for Charlie. Do you think Black is coming
back for you, or should I be worried today?'

Dr Quigg spoke up. 'Perhaps I'm the D he wants?'

'Do you imagine Black thinks that Doctor is your first name? Or is that only you?'

Cyrus reined them in. 'Look here, we've got to get it together. He's slipped up once—Charlie got out. And I'm a 'C' too, you know. Black's only a man, he's not infallible. We've got eight brains and eight sets of eyes between us. We can out-think him and get on top.'

'Do you really think that bath contraption was meant to do Charles in?' Inspector Vail asked sceptically.

'You think not?' asked Dr Quigg.

'It just seems an awful...lot.'

'Maybe they shipped them folded up? Perhaps Ms Hedringer pulled the wrong lever?'

'Devilish design if it was.'

'Inspector,' said Cyrus, 'the bath contraption is something that took work and scheming to arrange. Black gave the room list to the MacGregors, so he knew who was going to sleep where. Sooner or later Charlie would have taken a bath, and that would have been that for him. Only Black wouldn't have expected his invited biographer to share his hospitality with his lady friends.'

'Now see here, Cyrus! You're going too far!' Charlie was red-faced.

'Don't be sore. Nothing meant. Just stating the facts as I find them.'

'What do you mean, 'eight brains and eight sets of eyes'? Have you forgotten what you said earlier? You said one of us is helping him out. Have you changed your opinion on that?'

'No,' answered Cyrus. 'No,' he said, looking around at them. 'I haven't changed my mind on a thing.'

'You're still shaking, Ms Hedringer. Please sit down.' Joan accepted the bench. Dr Quigg was all motherly tenderness.

The two girls had gone out for a walk, Joan needing to get away from the house. They sat for a moment beneath the canopy, the soporific sound of the rain on the roof a tonic after what happened. 'It's understandable. A terrible shock. It must have scared you a lot.'

'It did a bit. I suppose it did. I don't know what would have happened if not for Charles.'

'I think we both know exactly what would have happened.'

'Well, yes. A terrible thing.'

'Hmmm.'

'Please, Dr Quigg. Call me Joan.'

'Well, only if you call me Frances.' She put her hand on top of the younger woman's and gave it a squeeze of support.

Dr Quigg had suggested the hot houses, the tropical gardens under warm glass with the heat thermally fed from below. They ran the short way until they reached its door, sheltering under their jackets. It was a sanctuary of sorts and served so now; she found it peaceful with its butterflies and terrapin pools. There were parakeets and bright red tiny birds whose identification fluttered on the edge of her memory. They were shorter by a tail than a chickadee, and prone to swooping dives. They darted between the thicker growth, and the air vibrated when they flew nearby.

'Do you have children of your own?' Joan wasn't sure why she asked the question; perhaps she was searching for a softer side to this woman.

'Me? No. No children, no. I'd have needed a man for that.' She gave a short laugh which Joan didn't entirely understand but couldn't ask her to clarify. 'No. I was far too busy with my work, in any case. I've helped a lot of people, whatever they say about me. I've taught a lot of people too and made them better doctors. I can hold my head up high.'

Joan felt a little embarrassed. 'I didn't mean anything by it. I'm sorry, I usually say the wrong thing.'

'You're not really a nurse, Joan, are you?'

Joan said nothing. Told no lies.

'Why did you come here with Mr Bowers, Joan? Why did you come here really?'

It might have been a trick, but what could she say? What did it matter anyway? It took her a second, but then, why not? An honest question deserved a straight answer. 'Money. I came for money, and maybe a better job. Not quite the same thing, really.'

'You're no nurse.'

'No. No, I'm not. I wondered, you being a doctor, whether you might know. That it was just to get me here, a story that was figured out before.'

'Then what are you, Joan?'

'I work for one of Mr Bowers' television stations. I thought it would be exciting being a spy of sorts. I was to write it all up when it was done.'

'That's all? He brought you over here for that?'

'What else did you think?'

'What did you expect to find? Some society gossip? Things going on behind closed doors?'

'I don't know. Everything was paid for. It was a week away with the rich and famous, and it got me in close with the boss.'

'He brought you along to put his paws on you, whether you know it or not.'

'That's not it at all!'

'That's what he wants. It's what they all want. Women like you play them on it.'

'Frances, I think you misunderstand!'

'Do I?' Dr Quigg touched her leg. 'Don't worry dear, I won't tell a soul.'

'Tell a soul about what? What's there to tell?'

'You're nothing better than a whore.'

'Dr Quigg! I think I must be going.' Joan made to move but found her arm held. Dr Quigg wasn't finished, it seemed.

'Do you see that gate at the end of the path, the one with the red strip across the top?'

It was a sudden change of topic, and Joan was caught unprepared. She looked. She saw the gate with its warning sign.

'That gate stops anyone who can read and has sense from entering the glasshouse next over. 'Caution' is says, and all other manner of scary words intended to ward one off. I asked Mr MacGregor the morning of his death what it was we should take caution of, what lay beyond the gate in the garden, and do you know what he said?' Joan affirmed that she did not. 'He said that Black had had alligators from Florida transported, and he raised them here as pets.'

'I doubt that is true,' Joan said stiffly.

'Alligators. From Florida. In here. Are you not much of a believer, Ms Hedringer? Some of the final words of a dead man? Are you the sort who always doubts? Our host had a Greek bathhouse built and a man's head bashed in at Neptune's feet. What are we to think? What does that mean? Is that a messy revenge we were witness to, or some sort of human sacrifice?'

'I don't know what it means. I don't think it matters. Please, will you leave me alone?'

'Who is to say there are not real monsters wandering the next hothouse over? Are you brave, Ms Hedringer? Are you a brave girl? Will you walk through that gate and find out?'

'I don't know why you are talking this way. I think I should be getting back.' But Dr Quigg wouldn't let go. The older woman had an unexpectedly strong grasp.

'I tell you, though, I have seen crocodiles in Africa, and I have seen men at work close up. The monsters you should be afraid of go on two legs, not four, and they don't come with a caution sign. You be careful of your American friend bringing you all the way out here, little Joan. You be careful of Charles Fotheringham, too—yes, you be careful of him.'

'Charlie is noble and very brave.' Joan stood up to her.

'Noble, is he? Well, we'll see. I don't trust the fellow one bit. And I'll tell you why, although I'm not sure why I bother—you don't strike me as a girl who takes good advice. You see, the way I see it, if Lord Black wanted Charles Fotheringham dead, it wouldn't be too hard to arrange.'

'What do you mean?' Joan had to hear.

'Just that.' She snapped her fingers. 'Lives are easy to take. And yet Charlie lives. And we must ask ourselves why. He plays the hero and he reels you in. And little Joan dangles like a hooked fish: 'Charlie is noble and brave.' Oh, is he? Ask yourself why Charlie lives and why you are the one out here shaking.'

Dr Quigg let go of her arm. Joan got up and turned to leave. 'Pull yourself together, Ms Hedringer, and start to open your eyes. I fear this week is only beginning—but if you survive it, and I hope you do, you'll have your story after all.'

⊂⊠⊠⊃

'You are, sir, a man of the law. A man of the badge, if I'm not mistaken?' DB asked. Inspector Vail did not deny it. I'm afraid

DB had been drinking all morning. His plan was upstanding in persistence and consistency and extended through the then, past the now, and terminated at an undetermined juncture somewhere deep, deep on the other side of afternoon. He planned to get very drunk.

'I repeat, sir. You, sir, are a man of the badge and the law.'

DB was capable of jawing bitumen wisdoms while his mind mulled finer things, and it was doing so now. His brain rambled tranjecturally, while his lips spouted nothing but sauce. *Perhaps when they've caught, tried, and hung that bastard Black, or whatever they do to murderers over here, I will buy his island after all. I will pay his widow cents on the dollar and have her throw in the Scotch with the bill!*

Inspector Vail was testy, having split four games of pool with the Yank. 'I concede I am an instrument of the law—not that it does me much good here. Are you planning on hitting that ball anytime soon, or can I nip out for a pee?' The Inspector wasn't walking away from the fifth frame and he wasn't going to let DB wiggle out. He watched the fat old bugger jigger his cue like he was mating with it. The American had played a couple of very good shots despite his inroads into the decanter. There was that shred of doubt, that ribbon unwinding, that Mr Roly Poly was stringing him along.

'You are a man of authority, Inspector Vail, and I am a man of power.' Off the cushion into the side pocket. Rolled up nicely, thank *you* very much.

'Is this going somewhere? I mean, what *is it* are you talking about?' DB was now two balls behind.

'I'm saying we know each other. I'm saying we can speak frankly together as men of action, while those who don't understand us cannot.'

'Is that even supposed to make sense? All right then, I'll play along. What might be fermenting in your mind that you are determined to get out?' *The bugger will never make that shot; not all the way to the other end of the table. Hold on. Bloody hell.*

'You are sworn to defend and uphold laws,' DB explained as he chalked the tip of his cue. 'I am not commenting on whether you do.' He put the chalk back on the cushion.

'Are you accusing me or something?'

DB lined up the next ball. 'No, no. Nothing of the sort. None of my business, Inspector Vail, what you got up to in Hong Kong; I truly couldn't care less. What I *am* talking about is the nature of law itself.'

'Law itself?'

'Exactly. How does the law come to be? What does it mean? Is it, after all the dust and dirt have settled, something even real? Surely in your line of work such questions have crossed your desk.'

'I've put villains behind bars who thought the law was pretty real. And if someone sabotaged your presses or pirated your shows or didn't honour their contracts with you, would you be calling on the law? Or would you be happy to call that self expression? I don't know what you're on about, mate. I think you're talking a lot of bollocks, if you don't mind me airing my mind.'

'Honesty is what we do have, Inspector. It's a luxury of our predicament. A dish that is rarely served.'

'I'm betting all this law talk rubbish means you don't think it applies to you.'

'You're a gentleman worthy of your office, Inspector! But that is exactly where I am going. Laws do not apply to me! Bravo. But not me. Not just for me. Laws don't apply to any of us, anywhere. They're a figment of the imagination.'

'God, I knew it.'

'Laws do not exist—they aren't real. You cannot eat them or see them or touch them. Laws do not apply to any of us, unless we ourselves make it so.'

'So which is it? Where does all this sprout from? You don't believe in God? You're one of those atheist sorts that figures you're number one? Or is it your tax burden you're all concerned about? Everyone else should pay but not you?'

'I'm an honest, God-worshipping Christian American, as all of my readers know. But what does it matter what I believe? So long as people do what they are told. That's laws. But all right, let's do that. Let's forget about the afterlife, or, better yet, let's put all civilized peoples on the table. You've got your Chinese God and your Indian God and you've got Jesus Christ over all.'

'What, him? The Captain, is he? Did you ask any of the Muslims or the Jews?'

'No, I'm not forgetting them. Bring them all in. Bring them all. The Orthodox east, the Protestant sects, the animists of the Kalahari. It's a great big party going on. 'Don't do this, don't do that; stand up, sit down', but what if none of any of that is real?'

'None of it is real? So now we're having no God?'

'I'm just saying. I get, okay, let's have rules and laws because God said so because he makes the show. I get that.

God's game; God's rules. But just saying, just supposing, this whole God thing is a joke.'

'They'll hang your sorry ass in half the world for saying something like that. And your readers will be at the front of the queue.'

'Yeah, but they ain't here now, and I'd deny it straight up. I'm an honest Christian American with lots of newspapers, and everyone will tell you the deal. But just supposing, just pretend.'

'Just supposing?'

'Just supposing.'

'Just supposing you don't make this shot. I'm going to win this game.'

'Just suppose. Suppose there is no God for a minute. Then think it through.'

'Think what through? What does that have to do with laws?'

'Well, as it happens, everything. Like, what is going on right here?'

'It's a pool game.'

'It's a house full of murder.'

'It's a murder investigation.'

'Is it? It looks to me like it's more of a hunt—fox and hound, fox and hound, only us foxes have been herded together.'

'People have been killed. There are suspects and witnesses. The law extends here as much as anywhere.'

'But is it justice what's going on here? Because the law has gotten up and gotten out.'

'The law, Mr Bowers, might not always be just, but mostly it's doing its best.'

'Did Andrew Sterling blackmail our host? You saw the briefcase yourself.'

'Even if he did, it's still murder.'

'The MacGregors' child—they never denied it. What was it that happened to it?'

'Needs a trial. Who's to say? There wasn't any evidence

that I know of.'

'Exactly the point I am trying to make. 'Who is to say?' Where was the law for Sterling? Where was the law about the MacGregors' child or about Dr Quigg's crimes or yours...'

'Or yours!'

'Yes, mine! Though I broke no laws! You see, Inspector, I have an admiration for what Black has done out here. I wanted war, yes—war was good for business. Do you know how many papers war sells? No? A lot, Inspector, a lot. I have an admiration for the man—he knows, like lots of men know; but he went further, he acted on the truth.'

DB lifted his wetted glass and saluted the air in the room.

'Here's to you, Alexander Black, you miserable murdering bastard!' There was no reply but his wheezy cheer. 'You see, Inspector, Black appoints himself arbiter of justice on earth. This is his kingdom, his island, he is God here, and we have a vengeful bastard on the throne. Old Testament coming home. Bow down, Inspector, bow down before him. Did he tell you to bring that gun? Are you to be his badge here? Carry his tablets around? Are you to be our God's right hand until all this is over, or are you another scared little man? Archangel Michael take a step over, your understudy's moving in.'

Inspector Vail thought DB was far gone in his cups. He half expected the fat Yank to fall over.

'Right top pocket off the spot, one cushion, and then in,' DB called.

Ridiculous shot, the Inspector thought.

DB thundered it in. 'I think that makes the game mine, Inspector. Now if you'll excuse me, I've got a glass to refill. It's been a pleasure, I'm sure.' He picked up the notes on the edge of the table, folded the money, and left.

Is that strange? It has to be, really. I mean, what would Mother

say? What was her name, the one we had? Catherine? Cathy? Or was it Kathy with a K? She seemed so old, though I suppose she wasn't really, clearing up after us all. But she had children of her own. What did her children do during the day? Beastly business, but one must pull oneself together—too embarrassing, really. Who would willingly sleep in a room cooped up with a body? It isn't dignified; no, it's not. What is she thinking? It's not normal. No. Not normal to grieve that way. She should pull herself together. We should get him out. That's what we should do. It isn't natural to stay there like that. We should carry him down into the shed away from all of us. Perhaps a word in her ear before it's done, in case she makes a scene. She's got to get things together. And not just her. Not just! Got to have order. Got to sort things out around here. No one is doing that. No one is doing what they should. It's wrong, wrong. All wrong. We should be sticking together and seeing it through until the end. That's it, that's the one. Sticking it out until its done. One big room, all of us, no one leaves, no one is allowed to go, we'll all be safe together. Yes, that's it. That's the one. Plan. Stick it out until the boat comes. How many days until Friday? One room, that's all. Got to make sure it has a toilet, I suppose. No one gets in or out. Why don't they see that? It's easy, really. What's the problem with them? Oh, dear. There she goes again. What is it she does over there? Why does she always go alone? What is the matter with everyone?

Eight green bottles, sitting on the wall...

Yes, it's a good plan. He's got the right idea. The others won't suspect a thing, and then we'll be free and clear. I hope she understands. It is a bit rotten, I suppose it is, doing this to her. But then it's the only way to be sure. The only way.

⟨⊗⊗⊗⟩

Go on, stare. Gawp with your moo moo eyes. But I know. I know what it is; I figured it out already. I know your little scheme, and I won't play along. Gawp, gawp. Moo moo eyes. I'd put them out with a pin.

⟨⊗⊗⊗⟩

6% battery left. No service detected. No networks found.

The bar went green.

Charon's iPhone network. One bar.

Do you want to join Charon's iPhone network? Yes / Cancel

<Yes>

Incoming message.

'Hello.'

Thumb thumb thumb.

'Cyrus?' SEND.

Nothing. Activity. Delay. Incoming.

'No.'

Thumb thumb thumb.

'Who is this?' SEND.

Delay. Activity. Incoming.

'Who is *this*?'

Two bars network strength.

Thumb. Thumb.

'It's Frances. Who is this?' SEND.

Delay. Activity. Incoming

'Frances! How nice.'

Thumb. Thumb. Thumb.

'Who is this? Who am I talking to?' SEND.

Delay. Delay. Activity. Incoming.

'Frances, you shouldn't have come.'

Pause. Pause. Heart rate going. Thumb. Thumb. Thumb.

Thumb. Thumb.

'WHO IS THIS! TELL ME! TELL ME RIGHT NOW!'
SEND.

Three bars network strength.

Delay. Activity. Activity. Activity. Activity. Incoming.

'Are you close? Am I getting closer? Are you there, sweet Frances? I'm going to get to you very soon. You won't have to wait too long. :-)'

Dr Quigg ran for her door. She turned the key and sank to the floor. Her hands shook and she sobbed out loud as she tried to turn off her phone.

⬤⬤⬤

'Rain's coming in. Wind's picking up.'

'Batten down the hatches, old son.'

'I'll never understand why people go abroad. This is God's country right here.'

⬤⬤⬤

Hush little baby, don't say a word, daddy's going to buy you a mockingbird. And if that mockingbird don't sing...

⬤⬤⬤

Why is he looking? I see him looking. Why is he looking at me? What is his problem? Little sneak. 'Hey, what were you doing in there?'

'Pardon me?'

'What were you doing in there?'

'You've clearly been drinking. I simply don't know what you mean.'

'Hey, you! Don't you turn away. In that Sterling guy's room. I saw you. I saw you, I did. What's that you got there?'

'Look here. You can lower your voice. I wasn't in any

room. I don't know what you mean.'

'I saw you! I saw you come out. What the hell is that you've got? Hey, come back here!'

'Are you all right? You're clearly mistaken.'

'I saw you!'

'What's the matter? You don't look well.'

'Hey, what have you got? Wait, I can't...Wait. My. I can't...I can't...My...'

'Hold on. Just breath. Help! Someone help! You're going to be okay. He's fallen! He's fallen! Quickly! Someone over here!'

<hr />

Hush little, baby, it's not your fault, mummy and daddy love you so much; and if you close your eyes and sleep, mummy and daddy will always be near.

<hr />

'Why did we agree to do this, Cyrus dear?'

'I thought the walk would do us good. Get out and clear the air.'

'These are the shortest heels I have, darling. Please tell me it's not much further.'

'It's a little narrow, and if I remember there's a trail that goes up very soon. Yes, here we are, that's it, before that rock. Be careful though, it's quite steep, and you wouldn't want to fall.'

'Dear goodness, Cyrus. It's a beastly cliff. Do we really have to go this way?'

'I'm sorry, Eleanor, it's the only way up, and you'll be happy you came when you see it.'

'I'm getting all wet!' But she laughed when she said it. The bruised sea, beaten onto the rocks, kicked spray into the breeze.

Cyrus smiled, a quiet elation. One thing you had to give Eleanor credit for, the girl was up for anything. 'You go first. I'll watch you don't slip.' There wasn't room for both of them. Sea lions jostled on the shattered shore like an audience at the intermission bar.

'It's a terribly long way down,' she observed.

'Keep looking forward. You're nearly there.'

And then they were. An outcrop on the headland, the mainland and Muig, Muck, and Aardshan across the short sea. 'Good Lord! How old are these?'

'Older than the Bible by far.'

It was a circle of standing stones, no more than a dozen in all. Tilted, rough, enormous wind-scrubbed rock, intimately spaced, the whole of it thirty feet across. How they had got there she couldn't imagine. They stood like mourners about a grave; solemn, observant, pious.

'How did you know this was here?'

But Cyrus did not answer her. He took her hand and led her, purposefully, to the altar stone, lichen damp, that lay like a table in its centre. Their kisses were impassioned, urgent, younger; he lifted her off her feet. He lowered her down, her back to the stone, his weight pressed between her spread legs. And there in that primal earthen space that fell between the sky and the sea, their transience became an all.

⌘

From the notes of Charles Edgar Fotheringham
on the Biography of Lord Alexander Black
Working title: *The Dark Isle*

When questioned about her previous marriages:

She smokes, chain smokes, those longer expensive Italian cigarettes—even harder to get in California, I imagine, than they are at the tobacconist here. She chain smokes but only occasionally raises one to her lips, and half the time the thing burns down. I suspect it's a habit she cultivated to look sophisticated at school or something she does to induce the assistance of attentive men. I count myself in that group. There are few who are not. I probably don't have enough matches to let me get close to those lips. I fetched her two ashtrays. The first she rejected; 'Beastly ugly. The thing makes me ill. Please won't you fetch me another?' There's no denying she's a stunning woman despite her growing years. She paints her eyes black with a thick kohl liner both above and under— overdone and yet it renders, I can't think why, a sense of the Egyptian or the Orient. She sees me looking and she knows. There is nothing innocent about Eleanor.

In her words, transcribed: 'It's something I've grown used to. The suspicions, I mean. The little people. The little people are always grubbing for something to bring you down. I don't blame them. It's natural, don't you think? We're all envious in our way of something.'

I took her back to an earlier age, to her first foray into film in the United States when she went over, as a young woman, from England.

'You were Elspeth Tennant. Your family sent you away to school. Your father worked in the Civil Service.'

The comment didn't please her. It was DB who'd told me—he's got a head full of useless facts about his Hollywood actresses.

'A different life, Mr Fotheringham. And your facts need sharpening. I went over for theatre, and pictures came later. I danced, back in the day.'

I reminded her of the letter, which I read from my transcription.

Eleanor Grace. Hollywood starlet. Black widow spider. Three husbands already you've seen to their graves and from each won a burgeoning wardrobe. It is not everyone that gets to know when their last performance will come. I hope the reviews of yours are kind.

'That's a nasty piece of theatrics. Bitchy gossip. I loved all my husbands, they were all great men, but I only murdered the one.' She took a long draw of that cigarette as if she'd said nothing at all.

I choked on my soda water. It was quite the confession and entirely unexpected. I told her as much.

'Do you know how I did it?' I had none of the facts. 'I did it with a frying pan. Can you imagine? Extraordinary mess. I told the police he fell down the stairs. I'd never used a frying pan in my life until then, and I don't plan to use one again.'

Did she not love him? Was there another? Was it true then, she was after his money?

'Nothing of the sort. No. I was very wealthy by myself. No. Him. Him, I loved most of all.'

She seemed to lose a sense of where she was and stared off into space. I sat uncomfortably for a minute or so. I had to lift her ashtray to save the chair. And why, I continued, when she came back around, was she admitting this to me?

'We've all been called, Mr Fotheringham. Curtain call, and this is purgatory. It isn't Mr Black's book you're writing, it's St. Peter's, and he knows everything.'

DB gawped like a flopping goldfish on a carpet beside its bowl. His lips had swollen to an unnatural thickness, and his eyes bulged like billiard balls. He stared, side on, through a forest of ankles and could see dust balls under the couch. None of this registered in his frenzied brain; or if it did, he didn't let on.

DB was a dying man. Not that he didn't fight; DB fought until the end. He fought for breath, he fought for the air that his blood-choked lungs couldn't have. He vomited haemorrhaged bubble-filled bile rich in platelets and spiked with shout. He clawed the floor and dug slivers out, tearing his fingernails apart. He nearly split his shoes from kicking, but all his exertions were for nothing except to make his mess a little bigger and the scene a little more disturbing for those who witnessed it all. His bowels emptied—was that the smell?—and his pants were warm with piss.

Those who attended, and there were a number now, were uncoordinated in their assistance. Mr Fotheringham would have him sit up, while Mr Gordon wanted him to lie down. Ms Hedringer had a glass of water 'if he could manage it' and his tie and collar were loosened. There were calls for Dr Quigg. No one knew where she was. What was that? Was DB trying to say something? DB was signalling something. In the end they only got a wheeze, as of a car's tyre hitting a nail. It was a long, long last sigh, the rollers slowing, the last page on a late edition.

The doctor appeared.

'You're too late.'

Six of them stood in observance. A blackened tongue, thick as a toad, made it difficult to see into his mouth.

'He's eaten something, or drunk something,' Dr Quigg observed. 'It looks like he's been poisoned.'

Wendy MacGregor wasn't there. Wendy who cleaned things up.

'What shall we do with him?' DB's corpse looked heavy.

And it was then that they noticed the mantelpiece and the bottles huddled at one side. Somebody had moved them, and one was missing—there were only seven to be counted. There was something else too, a corner held down by one of the bottles. The sketch was pen and ink. An obese rat melted like a burning candle, dripping into a puddle on the floor. **D is for Douglas, dose and dissolve**, ran the caption underneath.

'That's a lot of D's,' quipped Cyrus, frowning. 'And what's with all the rats?'

Eleanor started to cry.

D is for Douglas, dose and dissolve.

Chapter 9
Who Is Black?

From the notes of Charles Edgar Fotheringham
on the Biography of Lord Alexander Black
Working title: *The Dark Isle*

The story I was told is so full of holes. I see that now, nothing is in its right place. I would have taken the job regardless—God knows I needed the money—but there's a jigsaw here with missing pieces. This was never a puzzle I would be able to finish.

Who is Black? I was looking back through my notebooks, searching for a hint of him, something I am missing. Was there a sign of things to come? What brought him to this moment? The questions that I'd drawn up to ask him, what use are they now? Arse-licking, fawning, mewlish paragraphs—embarrassing to read back on. Does any of what I know of the man explain what is happening here? Is there a clue that I missed, some grand project unfulfilled? The story folds. It gives false witness. One must pry the pieces apart to see the whole within. Or so I tell myself, because otherwise, what hope is there to stop him?

What of Black's early years? On the surface they read as idyllic; a young man, an only son, born to privilege and generational wealth. The Blacks tell it like a rags to riches story where brains and perseverance paid off. Back in the day, they were a farming family—tenants, not even owners—and one of them finds himself fixing looms for money when he can't put food on the table. Clever fellow figures out a better loom that allows twice as much cloth to be woven—smarter yet, he keeps the discovery to himself until his patent is a reality. He doesn't squander his money, he squeezes every penny he can, and is on his way to owning his first mill.

But that was a century and a half ago, and the world's become a changed place since then. What one Black started, the next consolidated and improved with takeovers and expansions.

The world wars were good to them, and they filled a lot of uniform contracts. They take their patriotism and go offshore, abandon production in the motherland, and lay plenty of people off. Hong Kong and then China— that was Alexander's hand—then Bangladesh, Indonesia, and Vietnam, and the looms are still going strong. High Street stores around the world source their collections from him. Worker pay and conditions? Not a lot of pages on those. Alexander was born with a silver spoon in his mouth and a fortune in the bank. On the surface he's the modern businessman ideal, a front page *Economist* boy. No hint of the sociopath, if you can overlook the fires of the Dhaka sweatshops.

He doesn't shed tears about social justice. He has no agenda to spread democracy. Nothing to hint of a burning need to right the wrongs of the world. He pays only the taxes on profits he can't place offshore, and he was a big donor in Thatcher's time. Rumours of shady dealings. A failed prosecution for buying influence. Public officials being wined and dined. But so what? What makes him different? China's opening, everyone is at it. What ties that to the MacGregors? Why pick on the little man, Sterling, who is after him for honest blackmailing? The girl stepped out from between parked cars. Why does he care about that?

School? Chatham House, a tea-stained photograph of a cricket team, but Black's name is not on the back. University? St. Andrews, not Oxford or Cambridge. Closer to home—but where is home, exactly? His parents are separated. He scrapes by with a third from a lack of interest, which appears to be a point of family friction. So the letters read. It is his late grandfather who still pulled the strings.

What year is this? We're into the seventies. Too young to know anything of war. Grandfather sees him as vacuous, and his allowance is cut. Alexander the young man is a disappointment. Drummed off to the Far East, the edge of a dead empire, washed ashore in a trading office in Singapore. In the heat with a damp shirt collar, he was allowed to grub and squander as he willed. Was that when he met Henry Vail? Vail wouldn't have been an Inspector yet, but there was a lot going on politically. Singapore's independence was in '65, but Hong Kong didn't go back until '97. What happened over there in those eventful years that the Inspector comes back here for him? They're of a similar age, certainly. And what of the company's records? Nothing except general concern and a steady accumulation of bills. No golden boy touch from Black.

But change blows down like a mistral wind to sweep dust from the lazy valley.

Black's grandfather dies—his namesake, and perhaps also his idol? Alexander senior passes away and is buried here on the island. What would that do to the young man? The expectation and pressure is gone—the bully passes and leaves a hole. Black's disgrace, his disappointment, is forgiven, and it appears he feels free to return.

And now Black finds a purpose? Is it revenge he seeks, or is he chagrined by forever walking in others' shadows? He returns from Asia, takes the helm of the company, and the profits get bigger each year. What's going on? Is the man just bored? Are there no challenges for him anymore? Is this a game? Are we nothing but pawns? Or is there something more?

DB, expired, took up a lot of room on the carpet and made a mess over much of the rest.

'You shouldn't touch him,' Dr Quigg said, warning Cyrus off.

'Should we leave him for the police?'

'Not that again, Mr Fotheringham.'

'I'm sure they'll want to do all sorts of tests.' Joan had a soft spot for crime show dramas.

'Of course we should move him. Don't be stupid. He's right in the way of the drinks table.'

'But the police?' Charlie persisted.

'If they ever get here, we'll tell them what happened. I think that's the least of our worries.'

'You really shouldn't. You'll get in trouble.'

'If I don't have a drink, I'll expire. Look, if another dead body bothers you that much, why not take a couple of photographs? Personally I think you're missing the bigger picture—getting out of here alive.'

Inspector Vail clicked a couple. Dr Quigg said her phone was out of juice, though not quite in those words.

Cyrus enlisted the help of Charlie and the Inspector for the task of clearing the American. It took no little huffing, puffing, and bad language. As Charlie remarked, 'It's a great deal harder to move a dead body than I ever would have imagined,' and DB had been a man of large frame. A trolley might have helped. 'Do you mind if I put a napkin on his face? I can't help but think he's staring.'

In the end, they determined to roll him up in the carpet.

'It'll keep all of the mess together in one place and be much easier to drag across the floor.'

They put him in the corner.

'Where's that Mrs MacGregor got to?' Cyrus asked. He was going to get her to clean up the stains.

'She shouldn't have left by herself,' said Inspector Vail, annoyed.

'I'll go and get her,' said Joan.

'Wait for me, Ms Hedringer, please.' Inspector Vail caught up. 'None of us should do anything alone. That should be obvious by now.'

'What's the matter?' Cyrus noticed Eleanor, quietly teary on the couch.

'I'm next, I'm next. I'm certain of it,' divested the weepy widow.

'There, there,' said Cyrus, arms around her. 'No good thinking like that.'

There wasn't a trace of it on Dr Quigg's face, but all she felt was relief.

CRXXXD

'Mrs MacGregor?' Joan knocked. The MacGregors' room was just past the kitchens. There was no answer to her call. Perhaps the housekeeper was napping? 'Mrs MacGregor?' She knocked again.

The door was locked. Joan, puzzled, checked the keyhole, but the key was not in the lock. *Where has she got to?* Their housekeeper was missing. Instinct told Joan to crouch down on her knees and peer in under the door. The key was there, three feet into the room, in nearly the same spot as last night.

Why do that? Why leave the key there? Why not leave the key in the door?

'Do you see her?' asked Vail behind her.

'Open the door, please, Mrs MacGregor!' Joan knocked far more strongly than before.

'How do you know she's not gone somewhere?'

Nothing moved. No noise. 'Inspector Vail,' Joan asked, 'Would you please open that door right now?'

The Inspector put his shoulder to work. Once, twice— they didn't make them like this anymore.

Mr MacGregor was present. He still lay under a clawing wet sheet where he'd been put the day before, the towel gone. But he was not alone. Mrs MacGregor lay beside him, holding her husband's hand. Mrs MacGregor was unmoving and pale.

'Oh, dear goodness! What has she done?'

To Inspector Vail it was apparent.

Joan went to the woman to try to lift her, but the Inspector pressed her shoulder to stop her. 'There's nothing anyone can do now.' And the Inspector was right. She was gone. On the table was a near empty prescription bottle, the cap upturned to one side.

'Call the others, Joan. Call the others here if you will.'

CRXXXD

The discovery of Mrs MacGregor's suicide at least solved the problem of DB's corpse.

'We had to put him somewhere,' Charlie defended.

'It's a beastly business. Just leave them in peace.' Eleanor told him off.

'We should run them outside. Store them in the gate-house. In case they start to smell or something.'

'Take them yourself,' Charles said. 'I'm not leaving this house for a minute.' And it dawned on him, if it hadn't on the others, that there weren't very many of them left.

'I say we put DB in here with them. We close the door. We can lock it, and that will be that.'

Cyrus had moved to the bedside table. 'What are you doing with that?' Joan asked him, recoiling in horror as she saw.

'Put down the candlestick,' Inspector Vail warned him, putting himself in front of the women.

But Cyrus had other ideas. Eleanor gave a wail and Charlie a groan while Dr Quigg winced. Cyrus took hold of the heavy brass candlestick and brought it down on Mr MacGregor's head. The sheet that outlined the still wet body spared everyone from seeing the result. His blow landed with a pulpy authority. The crack of bone; a dark rose stain. Cyrus swung a second time and then a final third.

'What was that for? The man was dead.'

'I read it in a book. I saw the play too,' Cyrus explained. 'There was this fellow, the murderer, who pretended he was dead and hid amongst the bodies and got away.'

'I don't think Mr MacGregor was pretending.'

'He certainly isn't now.'

'Why don't you put that thing down?' The Inspector toed the sheet. Most of them looked away. Mr MacGregor, beaten and drowned, had half his head caved in. He raised no complaint to this most recent affront and continued to hold hands with his wife.

'Pull yourself together, Cyrus.' Eleanor seemed embarrassed.

But something in Cyrus *had* changed. He no longer bore the cavalier outrage he had played or been before. He was agitated, suspicious, accusing. 'It could have been him! It might have been him. But if it wasn't, then which of you did it?'

'What are you on about?'

'Put that candlestick down.'

'Was it Black? Was it truly? Don't you get it yet? Black isn't even here! Has anyone seen him since we arrived? How does he do it if he's not here? Does he just slip in through secret passages? Does he take the air and then fly off?'

'It's his house,' Dr Quigg reminded them.

'Someone put something in Deebee's drink. It might have happened at any time,' Vail pointed out.

'Cyrus? Oh, Cyrus, are you all right?' Eleanor asked with concern.

But Cyrus kept going on. 'Who has pills and medicines that could be put together? Who knows about poisons and things like that?' He held them off with the heavy brass stick.

'You mean a doctor?' Charlie answered.

Dr Quigg laughed haughtily.

'Yes, a doctor. A doctor knows these things. Pills and poisons and things.'

'No,' said Charlie. 'No, Cyrus. Come on. Dr Quigg didn't do it.'

'No? Why not? Why not her? Why couldn't she do it? And even then, why not *you*?'

'You don't know what you're saying.' Dr Quigg was cold and direct. 'I think events have upset you.'

Dismissive, noted the Inspector.

Joan had the hangover that insight provides: The *doctor hates him for suggesting it*.

'I see it now. Pills and bottles for the lot of them,' Cyrus said, too loudly. He pointed an accusatory finger, Dr Quigg its target. 'A drowsy MacGregor would be easier to drown, while Deebee was poisoned, as everyone knows, and

MacGregor's wife died by pills. And *you* were sitting next to me on the boat. It was *you* that knocked him in!'

What is he talking about? thought the Inspector, and then immediately remembered the monkey. The screeching, clutching futility of Emperor Ming. The animal trapped, beyond rescue, tipping beneath the waves.

'You're a fantasist,' the doctor answered. 'Delusional. You should put down that candlestick and have a lie down. Perhaps we ought to give you a sedative?' Dr Quigg asked the question meanly, a withering look on her face.

But she had ill-judged Cyrus. He was in earnest, or had cracked, or convinced his audience and himself of as much, and he did not let go of the weapon. He backed out of the room, his voice low and mumbling, and then he turned and walked away by himself.

'Where are you going, Cyrus? Stop!' pleaded Eleanor.

'Shall I go after him?' asked the Inspector.

'What was all that about?'

'Cyrus!' called Eleanor, 'Cyrus, come back!' But she was only in time to see his heels turn the corner.

'I do declare he has gone.'

'I think he's gone nuts.'

'Silly bugger. What was that all about?'

They stood around MacGregor, with his head bashed in. There was no answer to that.

'And what should we do now?'

The large portrait dominated the west wall. 'Does he look like his Grandfather?' Joan asked, her feet drawn up on the couch.

'That's not his grandfather,' Charles corrected. 'That's the Black that started it all. Perhaps they look alike. I'm not sure. If you gave him whiskers like that.' The man in the portrait wore country tweeds, and a hunting dog lay down by his feet.

'Do you find that strange?'

'Strange? What?'

'That you've never met the man you're writing about?'

'Lots of people write about things they've never seen.'

'But not usually if they're hired by the subject.'

Charles didn't argue. 'I came up here to meet him.'

'How do you know that painting isn't him?'

Without moving, Charlie told her, 'The artist signed his name and the date.'

'There's not a painting here of him,' Inspector Vail intruded. The survivors were sticking close. 'I know. I've looked through them all.'

'And do you know him by sight, Inspector?'

'No, I've never met him either.'

'Not in person? No? I can hardly believe it. You were both in Asia together.'

'It's a big place. Believe what you will. All I've heard is stories. I only worked for his company at times. He had no Facebook page or anything like that.'

'You've never seen a picture?'

'Nothing much. One longdistance shot on a beach in sunglasses—some holiday from his wedding. So I'm not really sure who I'm looking for here. A guy in tweed with whiskers?'

'The MacGregors had never met him either,' said Joan.

'Not that they knew,' confirmed the Inspector.

'What do you mean by that?'

'I think, Joan, what the Inspector is insinuating, is that no one knows who he is.'

'There is only one of us left who claims to have met Black, who claims to know what he actually looks like.' The Inspector didn't have to remind the others that Cyrus Gordon had still not returned.

'There was a class photograph from Chatham School in the papers. The research that I was given,' Charlie said.

'And?'

'It was Black's year, a mass of boys. Black's name was

listed on the back.'
'So?'
'So was Cyrus Gordon's.'

From the notes of Charles Edgar Fotheringham
on the Biography of Sir Alexander Black
Working title: *The Dark Isle*

Thank you for agreeing to speak to me, Mrs MacGregor. I am very sorry for your loss.

I don't quite understand how I can help, Mr Fotheringham, sir. You said this were about Lord Black?

It is. It is. You see…well, as you know I was invited…It was arranged, really, for me to come here to help complete Black's book. Lord Black. A book on his life. A biography of sorts.

I see, sir. Well. Forgive me, sir. I can't say much about Lord Black, or even if I could, I might not be fair. I know little of the man except he hired us both, and what he's said of us in that letter that started it, and what's been done to my Robert since then.

Yes, yes. No, I quite understand. It's not easy, I know. I mean only to fill in what you think of the man and, if I may, to fill in some gaps about your own life. I'm trying to tie everyone to Black. I'm asking all of us and, if you prefer, I can treat anything you can tell me in confidence. I'm hoping that by understanding each of us a little better, we can get to the root of his purpose.

You mean the 'why' of it all?

Very well put. Yes, the 'why.' I'm trying to find the link that brings us together. I'm trying to draw the strings. Know him by his actions. Perhaps we can solve this riddle.

Solve the riddle before time's up?

Well...quite.

You talked to the other ladies and gentlemen, sir?

I have had frank discussions with many of them. Since this...since it began, a number of them have been quite open with me, though as I said, if you prefer we can talk in confidence.

And did they say anything about what they did or supposed to have done? About the things said about them in that letter?

Most of them talked of it, yes. In a sense of it.

You think they're all guilty? I think they are. I saw it in all their faces, Mr Fotheringham, sir. Yours being no exception.

And what about you, Mrs MacGregor?

I don't expect I'm any different.

I have grown to understand the weight of the air that precedes the call of the confessional.

You had a baby? I asked the question directly. I knew she wanted to tell. Given time, respect, and a cup of tea, finally she did. The infant's name was James, although he was never baptized. He was Mr MacGregor's son. The parents were married soon afterwards, but she was unable to conceive again. She was in no doubt that this was a judgment on what they had done. Little James was blind and deformed.

I still hear his crying. At night, sometimes I do.

I had to avert my eyes. Bite my tongue. Still, there were things about Black I was after.

How do you think Lord Black found out? How did this knowledge get into his letter?

There had been rumours. Local people.

They had found it very hard to get work. But Mrs MacGregor was not in any doubt that it was the angels who had told Black.

We are only getting what we deserve. I made my choice and I chose wrong.

The drawing was discovered late that afternoon, while hunger was on people's minds. It was inconspicuously placed, pinned to the wall in the hall further down from the locked door of the MacGregors' room. How long it had been there they did not know. It might have hung for hours, or only minutes, and might have hung far longer still without being found. There was no doubt. It was the same Indian ink, the same heavy paper torn from a spiral pad, the same skilled penmanship and comic stroke; they knew whose hand it was. Practice hones talent. Black was having his laugh. Something to fill his hours.

W is for Wendy, the caption read, *who went before her time.* The picture showed a prostrate rat, the body lying on its back, and the soles of her boots. In one hand it clutched a bottle of pills, just as they had found. Only Mr MacGregor was missing from the drawing. Wendy was lying all alone.

Chapter 10
The Clock Struck Seven

From the notes of Charles Edgar Fotheringham
on the Biography of Lord Alexander Black
Working title: *The Dark Isle*

Interview with Henry Albert Vail, former-
ly an Inspector of Police in Her Majesty's ad-
ministered Hong Kong.

*Thank you for agreeing to take the time with
me, Inspector.*

What's this all about?

It's my book, Black's biography that I'm writing.

*What book? There's no book anymore. Not since
we got off that boat. What are you really doing this
for?*

*You met Alex, I mean, Lord Black, through your
work?*

*I've never met him before in my life. He was
a big wig. His company owned a lot of factories.
Getting the labour to sew shirts and zips.*

*Then in what capacity did you know him? Why
were you invited here, for example?*

I thought your book was about Black? What's

the point of asking this? There are dead people piling up, if you hadn't noticed. How is this going to help?

My research suggests to me you met him in Singapore. That you first worked together there. What exactly did you do for Black in Singapore, Inspector? What did you do that he paid you during all your years in Asia, Inspector, even though you drew a salary from the Crown?

This conversation is not taking place. Do you understand?

There was a story about a girl at the factory— her father started to talk?

If I broke that recorder of yours and made you eat it, would you be any closer to finding a real career?

Is that how you handle all difficult questions, Inspector?

This conversation is over.

Joan's head was bowed, and she rested it on Mr Fotheringham's shoulder as they sat together on the couch. 'I'm scared, Charlie. I don't think anyone is coming. I think we're trapped here, and no one's going to help.'

Charlie's fingers reached for hers, and he took her hand in his. 'We've got to help ourselves, Joan. Look out for each other.'

'Poor DB.' Joan's shoulders shook. 'Nobody deserves that.'

Charlie consoled her. 'Yes, poor DB. And poor Mrs MacGregor,' he added. 'Imagine doing that. I wouldn't have thought she was the type.'

'Didn't you? Really? Oh, I don't know. She seemed awfully alone with her husband gone.'

'I never really paid attention. Feel a bit rotten about it now.'

'I was wondering, Charlie.'

'What is it, Joan?'

'About...about everyone. About what was said. What's happening, you know. Did you?' Joan started to ask. 'I mean...only...the others, and the letter...'

'What are you asking? About the letter and me?'

Joan worried he might be angry with her.

'Do you think it might be true?' he asked.

Charles Fotheringham. Suspended license. Driving without due care and attention. Did you even know the name of that girl you ran down on that road? Newtonian physics, Mr Fotheringham; for every action, an equal and opposite reaction. Natural law will win out.

Joan didn't say. It would be rude.

'What about you, Joan?' he parried, avoiding the answer. 'Haven't you ever done anything wrong? Anything you've tried to wish away?' He had noticed that she had a habit of touching her fingernail to her teeth when she was nervous, the refuge of the reformed smoker or the nail-biter who can't quite leave it behind. There was a vulnerability to the pose that Charlie found himself susceptible to. He was glad to have her near.

'None of us are without fault.' She might have been trying to make him feel better. Her voice was quiet, her words slowly chosen.

Charlie had the look of a migraine, and his fingers nursed the side of his head. 'What was it exactly the letter said?'

Joan pretended she didn't exactly remember. 'Something about a young girl. It mentioned a girl. The letter said you ran her down.'

Charlie didn't say anything at first. He closed his eyes as if he were concentrating. 'She just stepped out into the road. I didn't even see her until it happened.'

'Where's your snuggle bunny now?'

Eleanor's heart jumped. She hadn't seen Dr Quigg when she entered the room; the library had appeared quite empty. 'I beg your pardon?' The words came out as she tried to regain her composure.

The doctor sat quite still in the chair, a novel dipped in her hand. 'Begging's not necessary, Eleanor, and there are so few of us left for such manners. Perhaps we can dispense with the illusions and deceptions. I was only asking where that man of yours is.'

'I really don't know what you mean.'

'As you wish. Very droll. My only surprise is that you were all over Cyrus even before the letter was read. My instinct was that you were here to get into *Black's* bed and squeeze him for a few thousand pounds.'

'I beg your pardon!' For the second time.

'Whoring by any other name. But that's what you are, isn't it? Dress it up however you like. Was he meant to fund another picture for you? Was that what this trip was about?'

'I don't need to listen to this—you're nothing but a wrinkled old prune! I'll mind you to stay the hell away. You don't know anything about me.'

'Run along, then, run along.' Dr Quigg waved her book to shoo her out. 'Go find your snuggle bunny somewhere else. And when you find your knight errant, what then? Is Sir Cyrus going to keep you safe?'

'At least I *do* have someone.'

'Ah, that's it then. You've talked Cyrus into giving you what you need. I wouldn't be too quick to go chasing him, though. He's just as likely to clobber you himself. But carry on however you want—it's what you're best at, isn't it?'

Eleanor's vanity wouldn't let her go. 'You seem very sure of yourself.'

'Do you *really* think Black is doing this?' Dr Quigg had the smile of the preying prefect—*as if anyone could be so stupid*.

'If you've got something to say, spit it out.' Dr Quigg only laughed. 'And what do you find that's so funny?' Eleanor was aware of the fiendish hair pin that kept her own curls secure. More than once in a lonely spot she'd fended off eager hands, and she had visions now of poking the doctor with it and wiping the smirk off her face.

'Look at you. You really don't know.' Dr Quigg led her on.

'Don't know what? What is it with you? Your whole act bores me to death.'

The doctor bit her lip. Breaking bad news was not her strong suit, but she didn't go in for being soft. 'Have a seat,' she finally said. 'No, please.'

Eleanor didn't expect that. The doctor looked sincere. She considered the request and in the end chose to acquiesce.

'How many of us has he killed?' Dr Quigg started.

'Black?' Eleanor asked redundantly. And then, because there was no one else to talk to, and a part of her needed a friend, she started to add them up and answer the doctor's question. First, there was Mr MacGregor, she'd seen him in the pool, and Mrs MacGregor downstairs just now, so the pair of them made two; there was old Deebee with all his newspapers, such a horrible way to go. A horrible noise he'd made, leaking all over the place, and no one able to help; then there was young Andrew, or whatever his name was— why did they think it might not be Andrew? Eleanor had almost forgotten him, the young man on the boat who'd helped her onboard, the letter opener sticking out of his back. 'Four,' said Eleanor, 'if we count what Mrs MacGregor did.' She came up with the answer for Doctor Quigg.

'Yes, four, and almost Charlie, too.'

'You mean almost Joan.'

'Yes, perhaps I do. Nearly half of us gone then. Barely half of us left. What do you think happens now?' Dr Quigg marked her page and closed her book.

'Like I said, I've just about had it. You tell me. If you don't have anything worth listening to, I'd ask you to please shut up.'

'Let me ask you this, Eleanor dear, before you run off to powder your nose. Do you really think a raving maniac is hiding out there and hunting us down one by one?'

It was an unexpected question; of course there was!

'You mean Black?' Eleanor stumbled. 'But Black wrote the letter. He invited us all. Who else could it possibly be?'

'Oh, it's Black's place all right, and Black did the inviting. But how many men have you actually seen that are still alive and here on this island?'

Eleanor stuttered, buying time, not sure where the doctor was leading her. 'Well. I'm not sure what you mean. There's Charles Fotheringham, the Inspector, ...'

'And Cyrus,' Dr Quigg finished for her.

'Yes, Cyrus.'

'How old is Mr Fotheringham, would you say?' the doctor asked, tapping the cover of her novel.

'Thirties perhaps, late twenties maybe?'

'A generation younger than the Inspector or your man?'

'He's not my man, I've told you.'

The doctor curled a lip and lowered her eyes. 'How old would Black be, do you think? How old a man were you expecting?'

Eleanor Grace did some thinking.

The doctor, reading or pretending to, continued before Eleanor answered. 'Black lived in Singapore and knows a bit about Asia. The Inspector knows about Asia. Black inherited his title and came from money, a public school boy raised in England. Cyrus knows a bit about that; Cyrus even says he knows him.'

'What are you insinuating?'

'The best place to hide is out in plain sight. That way no one is looking for you.' Dr Quigg re-opened her book.

'Dr Quigg…it can't be.'

'Ms Grace. Open your eyes. I haven't seen anyone who calls himself Black, but I've seen two men that might be him. Be careful who you go kissing, dear Eleanor, it's a rough crowd that came over this weekend.'

The actress, hand expressively to her mouth, left without another word, and once again the doctor was alone. Dr Quigg turned a page; she took her time, licking a finger, fanning the rest of the text. She judged that she was about half way through, and was hopeful of reaching the end.

⬠

What sort of Inspector carries a gun? This is Britain, not the damn Wild West!

⬠

Look to the obvious. Look to the obvious. No need to get fancy. Calm down. She's got the pills; she's got the know-how. Can't they see what's really going on? That American fellow, look at him! Obviously poisoned, poor wretch. But couldn't MacGregor have suffered something similar? Maybe he was drugged first somehow. It was her word to say what happened—drowned. We were trusting her; it's clear now. Everything is clear. She's the one who gave the cause of death, and that poor Mrs MacGregor, too. Maybe one or two pills in her tea, and then who says it was suicide? She does! The strings lead back that way every time, always back to her. We took the doctor's word. So what am I to do? Watch her. Keep an eye on her. Keep your glass in your hand, don't put it down, and eat nothing from anyone else. Only drink from the tap, and whatever you do, don't be fooled again.

⬠

And if one green bottle should accidentally fall...

⬠

That's strange. This hatchet's only good for kindling. You'd need a real axe to chop up this pile.

⟨⊗⊗⊗⟩

'Cyrus, are you in there, Cyrus? Please, won't you answer the door?'

⟨⊗⊗⊗⟩

'A giant elastic band.'
　'Sorry?'
　'I said, 'A giant elastic band'.'
　'I thought that's what you said.'
　'It's what we need. One giant elastic band. String it between those two posts. That would get us away from here. One strong pull and we're out. Catapult ourselves to freedom.'
　'That's your best idea to date.'
　'Giant elastic band…or, better yet, a Cherokee war canoe. A Cherokee war canoe fashioned from a sheet of tin.'
　'Why tin? Wouldn't that be a bit tippy?'
　'Tin won't rust, and the trees are too small here.'
　'Good points, both of them.'
　'Cherokee war canoe and a dozen paddlers all done up in paint and feathers. They can row us safely back to the mainland, where I'll buy every man one of them a pint.'
　'Are you trying to make me feel better?'
　'Is it helping?'
　'I suppose a bit. Not really. This is silly, frightful stuff.'
　'Consider the alternative.'

⟨⊗⊗⊗⟩

'I'm not going to bed tonight. I'm staying right here. I don't care.'
　'You won't sleep a wink, you know.'

'I don't plan to. I'll be wide awake.'
'I'm going to lock my door fast. I plan to sleep very well.'
'How can you close your eyes with *this* going on?'
'My conscience does not bother *me*.'

CROSS

They were gathered in the drawing room. The force of social gravity acted stronger than anything else. The fireplace was fed from dwindling stock, and the heat kept the chill off the rain. Charlie Fotheringham warmed his legs before it, standing with a possessive arm around young Joan. Inspector Vail had switched to bourbon in memory of the late Mr. Bowers. Mr Bowers had been drinking Scotch; everyone avoided Scotch now. Dr Quigg and Eleanor Grace eyed each other from opposite sides of the room. No one had seen Cyrus for hours, not since the scene in the MacGregor's room.

There was a knock on the front door through the entrance hall, a relentless earnest pounding. The truce of normality fell apart.

'You get it.'

'The hell I will.'

The banging on the door continued unabated. All of them answered it together. The door was jacked an inch; caution in a siege. A sodden Cyrus Gordon was doubled over on the step.

'Fetch a blanket.' There was a throw rug over a chair.

'Is he hurt?' He was not.

'Where's your jacket?' Charlie asked. Cyrus was wearing only his shirt.

It appeared he had lost it somewhere outdoors, or perhaps when he'd set out he'd had none. Either way it did not appear to concern him—Cyrus did not answer.

'Where on earth did you go?'

'I went out for a walk.'

To the water apparently, or so he said—he had roamed

the coastline alone. As to what he demanded of the heavens he wouldn't say, nor would he share the answers he found. He was a shrunken Cyrus, a withered Cyrus, a man older by years.

There were looks exchanged among the others. *Do you expect me to believe that?*

'Why did you run out when we found Mrs MacGregor?'

Cyrus took the blanket, a chair, and hot tea. 'None of us is getting away,' he whispered. 'We paid the Ferry Man to bring us across these dead seas. I did not have the courage to face that truth. I didn't have Mrs MacGregor's strength.'

'And now you do? You caught a dose of epiphany with your cold?'

'Yes. Now I do. Now I do. Now I'm ready to see it through.' His head was bowed, and when he raised it his eyes were for Eleanor alone.

'Smarten up, man. I say, smarten up! You hear me?' The Inspector dressed him down. 'You're starting to scare the ladies. You behave yourself. Did you see anyone out there when you were about?'

'We are Argonauts, each of us, fated to never return.'

'Sit closer to the fire.'

'Dr Quigg, do you have anything? The man's taken leave of his mind.'

'No! No, don't.' Eleanor was between them. 'He'll be all right. He's home.'

'Home, is it? You're a right pair you are. Well, keep an eye on him.'

'Black didn't hunt him down?' the doctor asked.

'Why would you say something like that?'

'Just observing, my dear. Don't distress yourself. Just keeping to the facts.'

CXXXD

A clock struck seven in the morning in a room somewhere down the corridor. The drawing room stirred as light pushed through the drapes, the storm of last night having passed.

Taking up the herald's message and spreading the contagious dawn, the other timepieces of Taigh Dubh broke peace with the new day amidst an echo of hammers and chimes. In the drawing room, the Japanese lacquered moon phase clock gave a deep brass sumo chant. The castle roused.

One: Morning, morning, light and fresh air—good to be alive.

Two: Oh, I remember. Where is everyone? I'm safe and locked up in my room.

Three: What has happened? Has anything happened? I need the toilet. Is it safe to go out?

Four: Move the chair, turn the key, and peek under the door. No one there outside right now.

Five: Morning everyone. Morning, how are you doing? Did you sleep? Yes, I managed somehow.

Six: Is that everyone? I thought Eleanor was with you? What do you mean, she went back to her room?

Seven: Running footsteps up the hall.

Let all the clocks stop at seven. Let them chime no more. Seven shall live forever in my mind—as it turned out, not so long.

⬙⬙⬙

They put out her eyes. Why do that? Cyrus wept over the corpse. He could accept everything but that. They had put out her eyes. *Why do that?* No answer was forthcoming.

They had to force the door to get in to her. Her door was locked, the key on the carpet, not in the lock where it belonged. Eleanor was there, their worst fears realized—a bare ankle jutting out from under the quilt, its crooked angle and the bloody sheet telling them the truth right away. The Inspector lifted the corner to see. He turned away, white in the face.

'Keep the ladies outside.' But what was the use? There

were so few of them left.

Cyrus went to her and knelt down in the puddle, cradling her lolling cut head. Dr Quigg stood behind him, and they could all see now for themselves—the wound of Eleanor's opened neck; a cry from a throat that had been cut.

'It's an enormous amount of blood.' The doctor narrated the obvious. 'Whoever did it would have been covered.'

'Over here!' Charlie had found it—a boiler suit in a pile. 'Whoever did it likely changed right here, stood on this spot while she bled.'

'There's something else here too.' A folded straight razor sat on shelf, the sort old barber shops used. Despite its black handle, the thing stood out because it sat on a piece of paper. The Inspector used his pen to lift the razor blade by the corner. It was sticky with foul work.

'What is that it was lying on?' asked Joan. The Inspector picked it up and turned it over. One corner of the drawing was blotted in something other than artist's ink.

E is for Elspeth, the star of the show. A rat on a wheel, cut up.

'Who is Elspeth? Why not Eleanor?'

'It was her real name,' Charlie explained. 'Elspeth Tennant, before she went to America, before she got her name in lights.'

But the mutilated body that Cyrus wept over did not shine any more.

E is for Elspeth
the star of the show.

Chapter 11
In the Greenhouse

CHARLIE AND JOAN HELD BACK NEAR THE DOORWAY WHILE the Inspector went over the room. Cyrus was on his knees. He pulled and tugged at Eleanor's twisted limbs, untangling the geometry of her death. He laid her body out straight. Without getting up, he dragged the sheet from her bed, tumbling the pillows to the floor. He reverently laid it about her shoulders as if he were tucking her in. He folded it up so it covered her neck, but her damaged eyes bothered him sorely. Cyrus looked around as if searching for something and finally laid hand to a scarf. Going back to her, he blindfolded Eleanor, as if the day was too bright and she was napping. There was a tenderness in these quiet affections that Charlie, watching, observed. Ablutions for the corpse; a dismissal of anything else. *Cyrus,* thought Charlie, *is not one of us, if he ever was.*

Dr Quigg drew near them. 'Come with me, outside, please, just yourself and Joan. Just a moment of your time if you will.' It was a hushed request, cast not to be overheard, and suspicious because of that. *Still,* Charlie reasoned, *seeing as how the Inspector and Cyrus were for the moment absorbed, what harm could it do?*

CEXXED

Outside in the corridor, the three spoke in lowered voices.

'What's this about, then?' Charlie wanted it up front. He pressed Joan's hand to reassure her.

The doctor, in contrast, was agitated. She didn't know where to put her hands, still stained from examining the wounds, one moment lifting her fingers to her face and the next clasping them by her side.

'Why did you bring us out here?' Charlie repeated, not trusting anything.

Dr Quigg seemed to make her mind up. After a glance to the door she spoke. 'This is our chance. We might not have it again. You, Charlie, me, and Joan. Right now. Right here. If we're quick.'

'What *chance*?' Joan asked her. 'Dr Quigg, what are you saying?'

'I told you already'—the doctor was flustered—'There can't *be* a Black. There isn't one. It has to be one of them!' She looked at Eleanor's door, still cracked an inch, as if expecting it to open.

'You think one of those two did all of this?' Charlie was slow on the take.

'I told Ms Hedringer already! Haven't you been listening to me?'

Joan and Charlie looked at each other. In a sickly way, it made sense. When they'd heard the noise from above their rooms, who was it they had found in Black's bedroom? The Inspector had met them with his gun, and armed also with an excuse. Easy for him to say he'd heard someone snooping, but who else had been around?

'What is it you want us to do?' Charlie asked. 'You think we should try and take them prisoner?'

All they got from Dr Quigg was a short shake of her head. 'No. No prisoners. He's got a gun.' The alternative hung in the air.

Joan looked up to Charlie. Charlie looked down at Joan.

'We have to get away or kill them both,' Dr Quigg prescribed. 'It's the only way to be to be safe.'

'Black killed Eleanor, sometime last night, and you are standing here asking us to kill the others?'

'Can't you see? It's the only way to be safe!'

'But even if one of them did do it, you'd still be killing an innocent man,' he said, stalling.

'We don't have time!' the doctor pressed. 'Black is one of them! If we kill both of them, we know we are safe. If we don't, we are lambs for the wolf.'

'Why kill anyone? Why not just take them prisoner?'

'The Inspector won't give up his gun.' The doctor pressed something into Charlie's hands, something wrapped in her pocket handkerchief. 'We've already been out here too long.'

'But if I can get his gun...'

'And if you fail, then he shoots us all.'

Charlie opened his hand and unwrapped the doctor's handkerchief. In his palm was the straight shaving razor that had been put to recent ill use. Dark handled, silver crested, the initials AB engraved upon it. Alexander Black? The doctor must have taken it after the Inspector had laid it down. What was Charlie to do?

'How many green bottles are left?' the doctor asked him. 'Who's next, if we don't do this now? They're both in there, distracted.'

Perhaps if Dr Quigg hadn't used those words—green bottles—Charlie would have gone along.

Joan stood by him, supportive, neutral. 'You'll do the right thing, Charlie. You will.'

Predator or prey?

A moment. Another. The little girl that ran onto the road. How was he to know? *Vail or Cyrus?*

'There's no proof, doctor. There's no proof. And there's at least one innocent man in there.' The razor blade shook in his hand.

Dr Quigg reached into her pocket and took out a mobile phone. She turned it on.

Searching for service... Searching for service... No service found.

'What does that mean?' asked Charlie.

Network found. Charon's iPhone. Do you wish to join?

'What does that mean?'

'It means he's here, Mr Fotheringham. There's no time. You must act!'

There was a noise at the door. 'There you all are,' said the Inspector, and the moment, like that, had passed.

From the notes of Charles Edgar Fotheringham
on the Biography of Sir Alexander Black
Working title: *The Dark Isle*

I don't know quite how to file this interview. Dr Quigg agreed to it, yet was unwilling to answer the questions. She deliberately deflected all forms I employed to bring her back to the point. The topic to which I returned again and again was her experience in medical research. What brought her to this island? How does she know Black? Might she have met him? I pursued this line, burrowing for answers, and not unreasonably it would seem, for is it not implied quite directly, being the substance of Black's accusation?

Dr Frances Quigg. Entrusted with the care of the vulnerable, your treatments killed and maimed. Instead of repentance you built a career. A work ethic is the only one you have. You and Mr Sterling should talk.

Black's words. Otherwise why would Black care? Where had she been working around the time of Black's parents' death? Was that the connection? Or his grandfather? That had been the catalyst for Black's rejuvenation.

Fallooning around the Orient, a wastrel of fortune one minute, heir to it all in a stroke. Was Quigg indirectly responsible, or instrumental somehow? I could not *make* her answer, but then why did she consent to talk? Sentimental dreamery, half of it likely made up. If I were a medical man, I would say the woman is losing her grip.

In the house in Natal we grew roses, white roses. I remember the roses the best. They grew out of a brick-red dirt, roses by themselves, kept apart, all down one side of the house. It was my job to pull off the aphids, all the aphids. Mother gave that job to me, but like most children I had no patience, and she'd have to make me do it again. When Julia was older—Julia was my sister—when Julia was older she was allowed to help. It was important and it had to be done well. Pick, pick, pick. Every day. You would think the little animals would learn from the mess, the squashed remnants of their siblings smeared on the stems You would think that to walk over your family's remains would tell you it was a bad idea. But not them. Not the aphids. The didn't have the brains. On and on, every day they came, reinforcements of them. Pick, pick, pick. They wouldn't stop. Those that didn't fall to my hands, the ants came and carried away.

This was growing up?

You don't know you are happy, Mr Fotheringham. Things happen. That's how it works. One day you're sitting there, your job at the rose bush everything and all. And what happens to us after that?

Dr Quigg followed the ivy-choked hedge to the hot houses on the south wall. The condensation, as it always did, painted a fog on the inside of the glass. Today would be a long day, a day where the sun barely set. Not warm, of course, like back in Natal, but the hot houses staved off the chill. Back in Natal, the fruit trees would grow and the vines would rise from the red soil of home. Nothing there needed the pretence of glass windows to create the illusion of fertile ground. Whoever had built this, Dr Quigg reasoned, pined, like her, for long-lost days in the sun.

Dr Quigg closed both sets of doors. The second helped keep the heat in and prevented the birds from getting out. The hummingbirds thrummed and the little red finches trilled madly as they gave chase to one another. *What to do? What to do? What to do?* they cried. Her thoughts echoed their song. She regretted giving the razor to Fotheringham now. She had shown her cards to the foolish young man and got nothing for it in return.

And what of the accusations contained in the letter that Black wrote to us all?

I don't know what you mean.

Treatments, doctor. Was he talking of experiments?

Did the letter speak of all the boys I stitched up? Did it talk to all the men that lived, that I saved on that putrid table? If you amputate, does it make you a healer or only a sawer of bones?

The distinction lies in the circumstances, obviously. Is it something that worries you?

It shouldn't worry those who merely write about things. It's only a concern for those of us that 'do'.

I'm sorry. I'm not sure I get your meaning.

But you weren't there, Mr Fotheringham.

How could you know?

Growing up in Natal I had a friend, a girl I roomed with at school. We'd gone home for the holidays, most of us would, and one Christmas she came home with me. Do you want to know her name? <I told her I did>. *No, I don't think I will tell you after all. I don't know why she came home with me. I can't remember the reason at all. I think her father worked for the civil service, he was back in London or something. She was my best friend, and we pleaded and begged and one Christmas she was allowed to come. Her name was Grace—there, I told you, though I said I wouldn't—and...* <here Dr Quigg was lost for a moment, as if absent in the past. I thought the interview was finished and was about to get up and excuse myself when she continued in a spurt>. *The gardener saw us. I suspect that was it. I imagine that's how it happened. Father had him dismissed within the week—no use for tattling tongues. Grace was sent back to school the next day, and she transferred before the next term. I never saw her again. They took away her letters. This was long before email. I never saw my Grace again.* <Here she paused again.> *It was very difficult getting work in Natal, and the gardener's family suffered. One morning all our roses were cut down—someone had visited our house in the night and savagely hacked them all. I can't really say I blame them. I remember how mother cried about that, my mother who never cried about anything. Silly things. Silly things, roses. Silly things don't matter, you know. They shouldn't, anyhow. The aphids kept coming; they didn't stop. The aphids even ate off the dead. Anyway, soon there was war again and we would lose. There's an end to all things. But not that.*

Dr Quigg was wearing her long blue dress, the skirt painted with yellow flowers—she'd ironed out all the creases. Where, she wondered, had her straw hat gone? The last time she'd seen it was on her dresser. Not that her fair skin needed protecting under the tilted glass roof. Parakeets cawed from up in the branches of plants brought from tropical climes. There were trays of lilies and stooping orchids, their roots mossed in hanging clay pots. Dr Quigg felt sweat bead on her brow the minute the hothouse door shut—it was the heat of a Christmas in red-clayed Natal and all the more welcome because of it.

A sturdy gate should have filled the way, but its solid bolt was drawn. 'No entry,' it told. 'Danger,' it cautioned on a second plate, and then, perhaps as an afterthought or sad untold experience, a third sign was screwed on below. 'Risk of fatality. Do not open. Do not say you have not been warned.' Dr Quigg peered through the gate, which today was swung open and stood pushed clear to the side. The path before her was open. A second greenhouse stretched beyond, and beyond that she saw a third. Who else had been here? Who had opened the gate?

And then Frances heard something behind her.

Do you know much of debridement, Mr Fotheringham? <Something to do with wedding nights? She gave me a withering look.> *No? What of septicaemia?* <Blood poisoning? I hazarded a guess.> *An infection, not really poisoning at all. What of Schneewittchen floribunda? No? There is so much out there to learn. I've always found it a little strange how mothers and wives like to grieve. They want a bullet or a bayonet. They want an explanation. They want heroism and a charge. Light brigade. Against all odds. King and country; defending the flag; liberty and democracy against the barbarians knocking at the gate. That makes it a little easier to take. Wrap the corpse in the flag. It is something to tell her children, I imagine, why daddy is not coming home. Some purpose to it all because they need a purpose most of all—futility is a hard pill to swallow. I deal in death, Mr Fotheringham. It is the family secret of my trade. Debridement is a cutting away of the dead tissue from a patient so that the healthy parts might live. Septicaemia is rife in warm climates when antibiotics are in short supply; the patient lingers for days. And Schneewittchen floribunda? Those are the finest white roses, Mr Fotheringham. There weren't enough roses to go around.*

Something heavy was causing the bushes to bend. Something moved through the ferns and rubber plants that hadn't been there before. Dr Quigg heard the rustle of leaves and the scrape of something being dragged. She walked, backing away from the sound. Serpentine and slick it sounded, following her, getting closer. The doctor realized she had passed the warning gate and was into the second hot house. The tree in front of her exploded in chatter and a dozen birds burst out. Dr Quigg almost stumbled—the fright it had given her! Who had left that gate unlocked? But she already suspected the answer. As she backed up the path, something slumped in the underbrush; a palm tree at the back nudged and swayed. Dr Quigg didn't know it, but mangos ripened; life in the midst of her retreat. The room opened up. A pond, a pool—warm water greened over with a film of algae soup. She knocked a bucket and the stench of necrosis rolled out of the slurry that spilled. Rotten meat. Maggots. There was no growl, just the slap, slap, slap of ancient purpose and the drag of a scaly tale. Dr Quigg looked around for an exit, but she had lost her glasses somewhere. An unseen claw, reptilian and armoured, stretched forward, deceptively slow.

⟨⟨⟨✕✕✕⟩⟩⟩

They sat halfway up the stairs.

'Do you think Dr Quigg meant what she said?' asked Joan. 'Do you think she really would have gone through with it?'

'She had no intention of doing a thing. She was trying to bloody *my* hands, wasn't she?' answered Charlie. 'She was pretty keen that I attack an armed man. I don't remember her saying that *she'd* do anything. What was stopping her?'

'She was right about something, though—someone *did* get Eleanor.'

Charlie quietened Joan with a warning from his hand. Inspector Vail was climbing towards them.

'What are you two lovebirds talking about?'

'We were just saying it's only five of us left.'

'There might be a problem there.'

'What do you mean? Has something else happened?'

'Where is Cyrus, and where is that doctor? Because another of the bottles is missing.'

Charlie felt his breath go away. The Inspector didn't say a word.

'You are quite certain?' Charlie had to ask.

'I'm afraid so. On the mantle, in the drawing room. There are only four bottles there.'

'How long has it been that way?'

The Inspector did not know.

Where was Dr Quigg, and where was Cyrus? The Inspector had taken the razor back after Charlie offered it up for evidence. 'I'll keep that. I suppose a prosecutor will want it at some point.'

Charlie felt naked and vulnerable. Joan clung to his arm.

'Stick together,' Inspector Vail ordered. The three of them searched the house. Cyrus wasn't in his rooms, which looked as if they'd been turned upside down. Clothes were thrown about, pillows torn, a side table overturned. 'I don't see any signs of blood,' said the Inspector, and neither did Charlie or Joan.

Nothing answered their repeated calls but the steady chime of clocks, and from every direction eyes followed their progress—the gentile philanthropy of generations of Blacks captured in oil.

'We should look over there,' suggested Inspector Vail, motioning to the leadened glass panes of the hot houses. He wasn't the only one to have noticed the doctor liked her walks.

There was someone there, yes there was, there was someone, she was sure! Someone standing by the doorway at the other end of the path.

'Hello? Hello!' Dr Quigg cried out, lifting one arm and waving. Damned if she hadn't dropped her spectacles, but the person—she was sure it had been a person—had evidently turned and gone.

She spun again, for a moment confused, unsure of the direction she was facing. There was the path—the first or the second?—and there was the pond by the tree. The birds broke again from a high canopy like a bouquet of flowers from a cannon. They startled her, frightened her, as they cawed and hooped, distracting her for a moment, and the rapid scrape of scaly feet went unheard behind.

They arrived at the main doors to the greenhouse.

'Someone has chained these shut.' The Inspector had his revolver drawn.

'What are you going to do? Shoot them off? Get a pry bar, why don't you?'

'Hang on a minute. There's another door round here.'

The side door opened with a turn, and they went in together, huddled, immediately warm, uncertain of what they were looking for and unprepared for what they found.

'Good God! What is that?'

It was Dr Quigg, or some part of her. Much of a thigh and the leg below the knee, encumbered with a floral blue dress. A trail of gore stained the brickwork that made up the herringbone pattern of the floor, they followed it down the path, the occasional morsel left for the delicacy of the chirping fluttering birds. At the end of their view was a brewing pond covered in a layer of algae film.

'What could possibly have done this to a person?' Charlie prodded the familiar shoe.

'There's something moving in the water.'

A tail crested then sank below. 'It's a bloody great crocodile!' But Inspector Vail was slightly off in his appraisal. *Alligator mississippiensis*, of which Taigh Dubh's specimen was a member, hailed from Florida and the Everglades, not the African Nile.

They looked around. Had Dr Quigg run this way trying to escape? Had she found the way locked from the outside? Had the creature closed her in?

'Why don't you kill it? Use the gun,' Joan urged.

Charlie's stomach turned.

Inspector Vail considered his answer, of which many came to his head. 'I'm not sure I could,' he said at last. 'Besides, what good's it going to do for her?'

They returned by the same route. It was there on a side table, just when you walked into the place. Had it been there when they came in? They hadn't noticed it when they'd entered the greenhouse, true, but the potted plant that held it down obscured it from the door side. It was a piece of paper. A piece of bonded art paper, heavy enough and thick enough to take a pen and ink. In size the sketch was a quarter sheet and torn from a spiral pad. They were familiar with its kind.

F is for Frances, felled by a toothache.

The drawing, mostly inked out, might have been set in a new moon swamp. Sandwich rack teeth were all that was visible around a little mouse.

F is for Frances felled by a toothache.

Chapter 12
A Telephone Call

'WOULD YOU MIND VERY MUCH, INSPECTOR, IF I KEPT THIS for my book?' Charlie slipped the drawing into his notes.

'Poor Dr Quigg, what a way to go.' Joan was full of sighs.

Outside the greenhouses, it was cooler and not only because of the rain.

'It occurs to me,' the Inspector began, 'that we've rather overlooked that place.' They were walking back, migrating, if they didn't know it, to the drawing room where it all began. 'We searched the house and across the island for a place that Black might lie low. We became quite dismissive, early on, that he was in hiding away from the house.'

'I think I see what you're suggesting, Inspector.'

The outdoors was cold and wet. Not like a nice warm covered garden within mere feet of the house.

'I suppose it is possible.'

'Well *someone* left the path gate open and *someone* chained the front door.'

'Poor Dr Quigg.'

'You've said that already.'

'What a way to go.'

☾⊗⊗⊗☽

Cyrus roamed the house. Decanter in one hand and golf club in the other, he lurched from room to room. The pool table with its interrupted game and a dead cigar on a plate. A moon phase clock told of a waning behind the clouds and rain. He rolled round the door frame and spied up the hall, ear cocked for the reaper that might come for him with a squeak of the hardwood floor. He passed the door to the room holding Andrew Sterling. He passed the door holding the MacGregors and DB wrapped up in his gory carpet. Cyrus stood at the bottom of the stairs and rested an elbow in the banister rail, its post carved to look like a nut. He rested an elbow and thought of Eleanor upstairs. He rested an elbow and he wept.

Not going to get me. Bastarding proles! He looked down the hall to the drawing room. He recalled the burden of dragging Douglas Bowers III and the tremendous weight of the man. One by one, they had gone too quietly, supplicant, into the night. Not him, they wouldn't. *Bastarding gypsies! Come out and fight like a man!*

Cyrus, decanter in one hand and golf club in the other, heard the telephone ring.

Joan turned her ankle on a loose path stone, yards from the steps to the house. Charlie tried to grab her, but she went down rather hard.

'You've scraped your knee.' And indeed, her stocking was torn, her knee bleeding. 'Can you stand?'

She could, but she was limping. Her ankle was having trouble taking weight. 'Will you help me back to my room please, Charlie? I'm going to have to change.'

It wasn't far. 'Lock your door, Joan, and wait for me to come back.' He went looking for the doctor's bag.

The telephone rang on. He hadn't heard it ring since he arrived, but now it trilled with youthful zeal. Cyrus had only one thought; someone was on the other end.

⬤

The Inspector opened the chamber of his revolver and spun it to test the mechanism. It closed with a reliable engineered click. He didn't return the gun to his pocket.

⬤

Cyrus approached the drawing room, pulled by a silver thread. Three massive mullioned bay windows stuffed with drapery, and at their centre a delicate table with a telephone upon it. *Tring tring tring* it rang, the hand piece shaking to the beat. He looked about him, but there was no one in sight, and the telephone refused to stop.

'Hello?' he said, picking it up; nothing but silence in his ear. 'Who is this? Who is there?'

The fire axe swung, splashing blood up the cabinets, Japanese lacquer now needing cleaning.

The golf club fell and bounced off the floor, chipping the decanter on the way. A pool of good whisky was spilled and lost, diluting the puddle of blood. A piece of paper was released above him, which landed on Cyrus's chest.

G is for Gordon, careless at shaving. The decapitated rodent in the drawing was missing one half of its face.

G is for Gordon
careless at shaving.

⬤⬤⬤

What was that noise?

⬤⬤⬤

It's stopped. The telephone has stopped.

⬤⬤⬤

It sounded like it was coming from downstairs.

⬤⬤⬤

Inspector Vail held his weapon arm up, keeping to cover as he approached. *There. What is that?* Cyrus on the floor, where the gruesome evidence on display dispelled doubt that he was faking. And an axe. *An axe!* That settled it. He had everything he needed to know.

'I know you!' the Inspector shouted. 'I know you now. You won't get away with any of this!'

He felt the bullet hit him like a punch, landing beneath his ribs. He touched it with tenderness, surprised, a little pain; a stain ballooned across his white shirt.

'I figured it out,' he mumbled, dropping his gun, unable to control his hands.

'Please,' he said, his voice a whisper, looking his killer in the eyes. He was shot in the face from three feet.

⬡

Gunshot! That was a gunshot. <Bang!> *Oh, dear God, not again.*

⬡

Joan stood up from the edge of her bed. There was only silence in the house. She would have liked to change, to get out of her silly red dress wet from exploring and into some warm safe clothes. She would have liked to go to sleep and rest and wake up somewhere else. But it was too late now. It was all too late. She stole from her room and she fled.

⬡

Charles Fotheringham poured himself a drink from the tray; it felt like the right thing to do. There lay Cyrus Gordon in a tangle, half of his head broken in. There was Inspector Vail, spread on his back, his revolver lying cold on the floor. ***H is for Henry, too slow on the trigger,*** proclaimed the illustration pinched between the man's fingers. The drawing was of a rat in a policeman's hat cleaning a blunderbuss, the rodent gnawing on its wide chamber.

H is for Henry
— too slow —
on the trigger.

Charles Fotheringham leaned on the stock of the shotgun once owned by the gillie, MacGregor. He toasted their memory; first Cyrus, then the Inspector, feeling nothing inside him but the void. *What a sorry mess this has become.* But there was still Black's book that needed finishing.

The last two green bottles commanded the mantle. Charles smashed them aside with the barrel of the gun and then he saw her looking at him. She was outside. Through the window she was watching him, her red dress catching his eye despite the glare off the glass. She stepped back, discovered, too late. She raised her empty hands, supplicant, trembling; she stepped back, shaking her head at him.

'No.' He could read her lips if not hear her voice. 'No,' she said again.

'Joan!' he cried, but she turned and ran. 'Joan!' he shouted again.

Chapter 13
One Green Bottle

CHARLES EDGAR FOTHERINGHAM OPENED THE FRONT DOOR and went out onto the step. 'Joan!' he called into the rain, which all but drowned him out. There she was, a flash of red just going round the corner of the building. Joan did not stop or reply.

Run, rabbit, run.

Charles took the time to do up his jacket and retie a loose boot lace. She had gone around the back; or if she was mad, she had run out along the coast path. He went to find out.

'Joan, come back here!' She had cut across the field out front, its rolled golf greens now puddled. She was running from him, panicked, tiring, favouring her left leg. The ankle must be swollen and sore, every step must be causing her pain. If she stopped, she would quickly freeze from the cold; she couldn't keep up like this. He walked after her, long tireless strides, his cap pulled low to keep the rain from biting into his eyes.

Run, rabbit, run. Please stop and I'll explain to you. I'm the only one that can keep you safe.

He crossed the shrunken golf course with its bent and blustery flags surmounting the green, and now close to the bay he could see the white caps churn. Spray, frothed, caught on the wind, and hurled itself towards shore. A sole figure running in a scarlet dress, two hundred yards in front. A solitary splash of colour in this god-forsaken place. She looked like a tattered flag of revolution, its resistance snapping in the gale.

He did not hide. He tried again to light a cigarette, but every match blew out. Joan looked back. He could see her stop and turn, and he raised an arm and waved to her. She shifted and stumbled on. *Run, rabbit, run.* There is nowhere to go, no burrow in which to hide. *I will keep you safe, dear Joan. We don't have to die.*

Black was mostly right.

Charles Fotheringham. Suspended license. Driving without due care and attention. Did you even know the name of that girl you ran down on that road? Newtonian physics, Mr Fotheringham; for every action, an equal and opposite reaction. Natural law will win out.

He had thought about it a lot. About the woman in the car with him at the time, the married woman that had to leave. About his hand upon her leg and his attention up her skirt—neither on the wheel where they should have been. The punching thud of hitting the girl a split second before she came through the windscreen. Of how she puffed silent words, bubbled red mucus on her lips. He'd had friends in the Gulf War that went like that; punctured lungs no longer any use. He knew there was nothing to be done. He'd held her hand, the little girl, held her hand through those failed breaths while all about him was steaming radiators and his lover slipping away.

'She just stepped out, officer.'

'Are you all right, sir?'

'Yes, I think I'm fine.'

'Young un's on the way to school. I'll need you to blow into this tube.'

'Joan! Come back, Joan! Where are you going?' But Joan pushed on instead.

The coastal path was rocky and rough, and it got worse as it began to rise. It strung out to an exposed peninsula where a stone circle crowned the headland. Joan fell down—he saw her stumble. He saw her pick herself up. Poor thing must be terribly frightened. But she'd understand when he caught up.

Black was mostly right.

Did you even know the name of that girl you ran down on that road?

Of course he knew it. He'd had to stand in the dock, give evidence on the Bible, and wonder why her parents were not there. Business interests in the colonies. It had made the lying that much easier, not having those eyes looking at you. And Black had known—of course he had known—exactly who he was hiring for his book. The car and the sound and the windscreen exploding was on top of him when he learnt of the job. It was his fate. Everything was fate. This was why he hadn't died in the war.

'Come on, Joan! There's nowhere to go. Wait up and I'll be with you in a moment!'

He marched on, long consuming strides, eating up the yards. The coastal path started to climb, to lift itself above the rocks. *Run, rabbit, run.* The red dress was occasionally visible, each time closer than the last.

And then she was gone.

'Joan?'

The path levelled off, having come round the outcrop, and was visible for hundreds of yards. Nothing stood up from the low scrubbed heather, and there were only a few rocks for cover.

'Joan?' He raised his voice—and the gamekeeper's gun he had taken from DB's room.

She was gone. Evaporated. The wind blew strong, and he had to hold onto his hat. He turned back, expecting to see her, maybe doubling back, and after a few moments he spotted her.

But she was below.

Down, down. Sixty feet or more. Down on the dark rocks below, a bent broken heap in the surf. The path had come close to the edge; had she stumbled or tripped? Or— no!—had she stepped off herself?

'Joan!' he called to her. He got as close as he could, and with the fear upon him, he crawled on his belly to the ledge. She was down there, twisted, shifted by a high wave, white arms and a red dress amongst the kelp. 'Joan!' he cried, and the growl of the sea wind caught the word as it was spoken. Flotsam on the tide. Charles looked for a way to get down and reach her, but short of jumping there was none. He would have to walk back to the beach by the bay and make his way around at low tide. The sea broke in, impatient for the sacrifice. Charles had no doubt; she was gone.

⬤⬤⬤⬤

He cradled the gun, clinging to it as if for heat. The stone circle of ancient purpose was poor shelter for a man in a storm. When it grew dark, he went back to the house.

⬤⬤⬤⬤

There was a light on in the drawing room. He saw it through the window when he was still far off. It beckoned like a lighthouse amongst the shadows and the crags.

⬤⬤⬤⬤

Charles heard it from the courtyard, coming through the walls. It was still a tiny sound to his ear, but it grew as he drew close. There was a band! Not a record but an orchestra playing; it must be just inside the door. He slipped the latch and turned the handle and suddenly it was loud. Yes! An orchestra of twenty or more, horns and drums and flutes, all in time and merry as a cake of Germanic-sounding tone. The orchestrion played on.

Charles found the dead man at the bottom of the stairs leading from the drawing room to above. He did not recognize him immediately, but the portraits on the walls gave a clue. The man was hanging by the neck from a rope, his feet a few inches off the floor.

'Lord Black, I presume?' The dead man did not answer.

The drawing pinned to the man's chest confirmed his suspicions. *I is for Ian, who knew knot the answer.* Lord Alexander Ian Black. The dead man was his host and his employer. The rat in the drawing dangled from a rope. Musical notes suggested a soundtrack.

And so we meet at last, thought Charlie. *I've almost finished your book.*

I is for Ian
who knew knot
the answer.

⟨⊗⊗⊗⊗⟩

The orchestrion, Charlie discovered, was on a loop. Once finished it would fall silent, pause as the belts reset themselves, and then continue to repeat the last piece. In his room the music was not an intrusion; on the contrary he found in it peace.

⟨⊗⊗⊗⊗⟩

Charlie took a seat at his desk. He laid out all the drawings he'd managed to collect and all the pieces of green bottles he'd salvaged. His fingers were stained with the ink he'd used to write his notebooks. The colour matched the ink on the drawings, if anyone cared to look.

What can you possibly say to the policemen? But he knew he had no intention of talking. What was life but borrowed time? Every day he had spent in the war.

Charlie ran himself a hot bath. He got in and released the lever.

THE END

Epilogue

YOU ARE READING THIS, MY DEAR, BECAUSE I AM DEAD AND my estate has bequeathed this letter to you. It came with instructions—*To be read in private*—I like to think that you have obliged. I would add another request now; that when you have finished, you sleep a night on its contents before deciding what to do. Call it an old woman's whimsy.

Do not grieve for me, your grandmother; mine was an interesting life. I am gone, yet I came to know you. I played with you growing up. Those were my happiest days. Mine was a life truly blessed. You and your mother were a joy to me every day I had, and I am only sorry she never lived to see you grow up into the woman you are. It wasn't necessary that you knew the lies and the hurt that brought you here—she never did, excuse her that. Life is full of its own injustices without the burden of carrying others'. *What lies? What hurt?* Let me explain what little I can.

He was thirty years older than I. Some say these things do not matter, but darling, believe me, sometimes they do. My family, I am ashamed to say, was in favour of him all the same. I don't entirely blame them. I can see why. If it was anything other than what it was, I would have been secure and wealthy and happy. I was young, but accepting him was still my decision. It was I who made that mistake. It was I who said yes to marrying him and becoming the second Lady Black.

He seemed kind at first, the first few months, until he became angry one night and hit me. I should have left, they tell you to leave—you don't know until you live it. So obvious. So obvious looking back. And it was only the start. He womanized, too. He scarcely bothered to hide it. I had turned my head before. He got away with everything, and that became our norm. He was a dreadful man, a terrible husband, but he did not kill those people.

What happened on the island was twenty years before you were born. And yet, my dear, has it not defined us? We who kept its secrets or who live to carry them on? For you were defined by them, though you did not know it, and now they are yours to do with as you choose.

I would read my husband's correspondence; I knew his email password. Andrew Sterling gave me the idea. Andrew started all of it when I intercepted his first letter. It was full of vile truths, and it was full of proof. He wanted money from my husband's pockets. I had Mr Sterling send all future correspondence to a PO Box that I arranged. My husband knew nothing about it. I learned much from Andrew Sterling. I paid him off in tiny bites, and he would come back hungry for more. There was power in the pretence of being my husband. People respected and feared him. Money has that power. My husband hit me, disgraced me. A divorce would have revealed my shame and only scratch his reputation. I felt a conspirator's thrill, and my list began to grow. If I was to kill Alexander—and I was going to kill him—why not Sterling too? You see, my dear, I wanted my freedom, but I wanted justice more.

You know the names. There were ten.

Alexander was going to sell the island. I had visited it early in our marriage. Alexander bragged how he would make all this money from a greedy media tycoon, a Mr Douglas Bowers III. I knew that name of old. I was five years old in 1975 when my brother went to war. South Africa entered the Angola conflict which was a cold war battleground. I needn't have been a lonely child. Is it important to know which newspapers encouraged the debacle, or which newspaper owners invested heavily in mining stock that did very well after the outcome? Why should we care when no one else does, my dear? And yet I remembered that name. There was a date suggested for the sale of the island; I had the beginnings of my plan, and now I had a timeframe, and the list had grown to three.

Alexander was vain, and I had to endure stories of his celebrity friends. He bragged of and envied the pandering letch, Cyrus Gordon, whom he went to school with. His autopsy confirmed the long-held rumours that he was indeed HIV positive—pity his poor wife. The man was a charming plague. That made four.

There was the movie star from near where he was born, who got ahead by eating her own. Prideful Eleanor. Alexander was a big fan. It was bad enough that I had to endure the repeated screenings, but I was encouraged to admire this murderer. It was an open secret what she had done, but entertainment demanded her freedom, and that's what the public got. For a while. My list was up to five.

I listened to the stories of how Alexander had arranged for a policeman in Hong Kong—the man was English and nursed a drug habit—to sort out his local problems. I read reports of the Scottish couple that had murdered their unwanted child. I lost a child before your mother came along, my step-daughter who stepped out onto a road. That driver got off with only a fine. A suspended licence in lieu of a life? My list was up to nine. And finally there was Dr Quigg, the resident surgeon when my brother was admitted. She didn't pay enough attention. My list had grown to ten.

They were going to show the island to Bowers during summer so he could see it at its best. It took me nearly a full year to put my plan together.

You have read the newspapers of the time? *Death on the Dark Isle*? *The Murders at Taigh Dubh*? And my personal favourite, *Ten Green Bottles*—I hope the copyeditor got well paid for that. The anniversary was celebrated, and then five years later, and now only occasionally. My husband was tried in absentia and found guilty of the murders; they discovered his boat anchored in the cove. They didn't know I sailed over with him; they didn't know he was dead before it anchored. The island was deserted as arranged, the MacGregors not due for two days. If I was to do it all again, I'd have killed the bastard onshore, as he was a terrible bother getting into the dinghy. I don't advise it to anyone. Taigh Dubh has a car, but I couldn't get it to run. Thank goodness the yacht was in the bay by the house. I put my husband in the wheelbarrow and pushed him in to await his guests.

They looked for my husband for days when it started, and the irony was that he was there all along. Behind the orchestrion under the stairs was a draughty panel that fit the purpose. He only had to be there a week at most—still I was worried he would start to smell. I also didn't want an embryonic curl if rigor mortis set in—I had to hang him later, you must remember, the rope already around his neck. They could do a lot with science, even back then, so I wanted the blood down in his feet. I propped him up straight and left him there. I was rather terrified when Cyrus brought his monkey, I thought the creature would sniff my husband out and give the game away. When I saw Dr Quigg push the cage off the boat when she thought no one else was looking, I didn't say anything. I know you must think me awful, dear, but don't underestimate the capacity for real evil. These people are but names to you, yet even now I can still see their faces.

Douglas Bowers III had a lady friend who took a helicopter with him, an assistant that got on the *Selkie* with him whose name was not on the list. The captain would have seen her, would have remembered her when the police interviewed him as they did many times. It was easy to arrange for my new job, for my role as Joan. I wrote to Mr Bowers as my husband and asked that he bring a 'friend'. The woman was an acquaintance and his wife couldn't know about her—would he do him this favour? He could pass her off as a nurse. Old men and their ideas. A hair cut and dye is cheap.

Andrew was easy. He was pleased to see me at the boat, for I'd been delivering him bundles of notes. The sight of me gave him confidence. With the distraction of the letter being read in the drawing room, I told him we should get this done. The sight of all that money made him grin. When he turned to count the stack I had handed over, I had the opportunity I needed. He was stealing what was rightfully mine. He wasn't a very nice person.

I was worried about the MacGregors—how obedient would they be, or lazy, or incompetent? Would they follow all the instructions I had given them? Would they lay the table and assign all the rooms as 'Lord Black' had requested? I needed help to run the house, and there couldn't be any witnesses. They proved to be model servants. Ideal for their tasks.

Mr MacGregor had no fear of a young woman. There was a fist-sized bronze Buddha I was fond of—I put it in a sock. I hit him on the back of the head and then pushed him into the pool. It was pretty much as the papers reported. He struggled a little, a part of his Neanderthal brain perhaps knowing that this was the last. I used the rescue pole on the wall, which I pushed down on his back. It was as easy as drowning kittens, I imagine—which, my dear, I would never do.

I felt sorry for Wendy. Wendy who went before her time. Her conscience was stronger than mine.

DB was easier and yet, in some ways, more difficult. I had brought the pills when I had planned the nurse ruse— it wasn't just aspirin or laudanum. Getting him to drink wasn't a problem, either; it was harder finding a moment when he didn't have one in his hand. No, the problem with DB was his explicit guilt, or the lack of it—he was a provider for the dark in men's souls. Is that the same as pulling the trigger? Was that blood enough on his hands? Did he really kill my brother, or was he innocent? Knowing what I know today, I'd have spared the rest and killed ten of him. That was my second regret.

Eleanor/Elspeth was not as hard as you might expect. She was a tool of the system, yes she was, but she had chosen and courted it. Do you know they raised a statue of her in a park along Hollywood Boulevard? They made her look twenty years younger. She would have like that. There is a conspiracy theory that she is alive and well and that the studio faked it all.

Dr Quigg I think of until this day and what her neglect did to our family. The wrongs that have been done in the name of science when stripped of its humanity! I had not thought the creature would get her—I was waiting for her to escape, actually, and I only locked one of the doors to force her to come to me. Natural justice did prevail, though; it is sharp, brutish, and noisy. Did you read the papers? They never did find the alligator! Perhaps it, like me, got away.

Vanity was another of Alexander's sins. I remember compiling the photographs and letters I was preparing for my husband's biographer. He loved the idea, of course. Alex put me in touch with Cyrus directly, and Cyrus was a revelation. Cyrus came up in a number of stories he thought would be good for the book. Of course we never met face to face. My husband was sick the day the team picture was taken but for a time they had been close friends. How many women, how many *men*, how many mothers or wives did he wipe himself in, spreading infection and disease? He was a pleasant devil and made advances to me in our correspondence. He wasn't without his appeal. He actually told us how he would like to die—went on about his axe. How could I refuse such a request? He never thought of a woman as dangerous—he was another one. Remarkably un-insightful, for all his intelligence, and selfish to the core.

Inspector Vail figured me out. He almost caught me; well, actually he did. I believe his suspicions were aroused very early when I was not included at the dinner to eat. There were eight sittings for dinner, plus the two servants, and ten green bottles laid up. I only managed a chair because my husband did not show up. Where was Black? they asked, unaware his wife stood amongst them bearing that very name. I could see Vail wondering, and when it came to the letter, why was my husband not charged? The obvious answer is that my husband was meant to write it, but to a man like the Inspector something else was wrong. Why ten bottles and not nine, if only nine charges were laid? So I was on his radar. Charlie, however, soon became the focus of his attentions. First us meeting him in Black's rooms, and then my staged escape from the bath—I thought that played very well at shedding suspicion on me. Forgive me, my dear, I ramble on, I talk to you as if you had been there. Where is the reality—in the coroner's report or the mind of a sick old woman?

A couple of the drawings I took my time over and completed before everyone arrived. I drew them at my husband's desk after sticking him under the stairs. They were an amusement at first, a distraction for me to keep my nerve in check—I was not without my doubts. I had not intended to share them at first, but when they were found! Oh, I took a degree of delight in the reaction. Cyrus saw just how funny they were, and that almost spoiled everything. Then the art experts at the trial who tried to link them to everyone in turn. Old school work dragged out for comparison, and I haven't lifted a brush or pen since for fear of anyone noticing.

I think the Inspector knew very early that it was not Lord Black who was doing these things. He knew it was one of us. And then after Cyrus went with the axe, his suspicions were confirmed. Only someone in the room when Cyrus spoke of it would presume to use such a thing, and Charlie had stepped away. The Inspector had his gun on me, it was that close. I shot him with my husband's revolver that I'd had with me from the beginning.

I left Charlie on the cliff. I had lured him out, feigning a hurt leg, letting him catch up to me. It was Mrs MacGregor's body down below, convincing in the stark change of dress. In my arrangements I had found a picture of her from a Facebook image. My hair cut and colour were set close enough; I wore mine down, since she kept hers up, so the similarity was not obvious. She was of a shape and size not too far off that my second red dress fit. I had brought two exactly the same with the potential for deception in mind. The night before, I had changed her and taken her body to the cliff. Poor Wendy, I let her hair down like mine. It was no coincidence that Charlie's glasses went missing—I didn't want him looking too closely.

And then there was Charlie himself.

You have seen the glories of Taigh Dubh? Its richness of furnish and design? And yet it is nothing against the mountains and water and the standing stones of the island. Theirs is an ancient beauty, a still glass of continuity into which troubles like ours pour without a ripple in reply. One walks in such a landscape and is given the joy of perspective; it is council with silent gods. Where now the highlanders, turned out of their crofts? Where now the Norsemen raiders or the monks that carried the cross? The Romans did not walk those hills that were home to the ancient Celts, yet even back then the standing stones were old, keeping watch on the Jura straights. What wrongs were done *to* those peoples? *By* those peoples? What rights and justices do we celebrate? One stands on the island and comprehends the value of mankind. We are each to our own. We are all flotsam. All the stars under heaven—what is ours, what is one? And we much lowlier by far. Waving grass before the storm. We are sown and grow and are cut. What is one? At the foot of mountain, above the water, beneath the cosmic all, I asked, where is justice, what of laws, who is the judge of right or wrong? Not you, not I, and, dear child, do you know my answer? The island has no such concerns.

I was under the stairs, the door cracked an inch, when poor Charlie came back to the house. He found my husband hanging and the drawing I'd pinned on his chest. I think his mind had had enough. I heard him run a bath. He was a kind man, a victim of circumstance; the war; the child running out that he drove down; and me. I had taken comfort in poor Charlie, I had used him as my unwitting assistant, and, though I did not know it at the time, I carried his child in me. I was alone in Taigh Dubh once again, and I cried for the only time.

I had made the crossing to the mainland once before. With the business on the island finished, it was time for me to go for good. I had been careful with what I had touched, but I took some time to set things straight. I have mentioned the diary and pictures. Charlie had made a sketch of me that was too accurate to remain. I wiped my husband's revolver clean, the one that killed Inspector Vail. I made prints on it from my husband's hand and left it in his pocket, where I presume a policeman found it. Joan's pill case I added to Dr Quigg's bag, which I found in her immaculately clean room. I collected the phones only because I wasn't sure if there were any pictures, notes, or taped dictations I wouldn't like disclosed. They went in a net bag and are ten fathoms down. I am sorry for that; I abhor pollution. That was something else the prosecutor couldn't explain, and I know it caused him problems. Wendy's drawing I redid and swapped it for the original. *W is for Wendy who went down a well.* That is the one they showed at the trial although, as you know, they never found her body. *J is for Joan who walked on the ocean.* I added that to the final collection. The search for Wendy MacGregor and a missing call girl called Joan was left open for years. Ironically, or not, it was Emperor Ming that rallied the public's sympathies. An enormous social media campaign had droves out looking for the monkey and hopes of its safe recovery. I put all the green bottles back out on the mantle, those of them that were left. I closed the door to Taigh Dubh for the last time and went out into the rain.

My husband's yacht remained undiscovered in the cove in which I'd put it. I had taken her up around the coast after bringing my husband in. I could not take her now, or how to explain my husband's arrival on the island? The prosecutor was happy. Its dinghy was small and the wind in the straight was fierce. It did not matter—I could not take that either. Joan had to disappear without a trace of escape. Even with a survival suit and vest it is a horrid swim. I did it for a second time. I cannot convey how cold it was—I would not have complained had I died. I was pushed in close to shore, and I might have perished from exposure, but as you see, I did not. Your mother was born eight months after. No one challenged the Black name she took, although we had not been intimate in months. And you were born of her.

I never went back to the island. The upkeep is not inconsiderable, but I haven't let it fall apart. I am giving it to the National Trust and the government to take care of. I am told that animals roam and that people will come back and live there—Taigh Dubh will be a hostel! So it should be. It is not really ours, one rich man's folly, it is ageless and belongs to us all. It pleases me to think of gardens raised and fish brought in from its shores. They've been doing such things for thousands of years, and there is a peace in knowing it goes on. The standing stones count the stars; our passing is but a glow.

And you, my dear girl, I leave you rich as a sultan—the grubby lawyers will provide the details. You have the truth, as much as I know of it; think of it what you will. A final drawing I enclose with this letter; a memento for you, I suppose. *J is for Joan who sailed away.* I think that is a better ending.

Am I forgiven? I answer to none. I care not. The question has no meaning in the dark.

J is for Joan
who sailed away

CPSIA information can be obtained at www.ICGtesting.com
Printed in the USA
LVOW07s2039251215

467859LV00006B/738/P